I0826608

Beaux Fest For The Wicked

A Collection of

Gothic Short Stories

by

Marilyn Brock

Skinny Toe Books

2009

Published by Skinny Toe Publishers

New London, Connecticut, USA

2009

First Edition

Request and inquires concerning reproduction should be addressed to the publisher:

Skinny Toe Publishers

27 Fowler Court

New London, CT 06320

www.skinnytoe.com

978-0-615-32817-1

Previously published stories

Half-Hour Nirvana / SNReview Summer Issue

Seattle's Best Neighborhood / Winter 2009 Miranda Literary Magazine

Cover Art by Alexander23

www.23photo.com

Beaux Fest For The Wicked

Marilyn Brock

For Darren, my beloved son.

Introduction

The American gothic acts as to redirect the shadows from a traumatic historical past into new designs on the present. Early American gothic narratives provided a catharsis from problematic historical circumstances, while the persistent popularity of this form continues to serve as a barometer for cultural anxieties. American concerns associated with World War I and II, the Cold War and terrorism can be translated into gothic narratives about invasion from others. Issues such as civil rights, feminist and gay liberation, and Christian versus secular models governing these rights, show up in stories that speak of hidden terrors in utopian settings. Joyce Carol Oates's *Black Water* is an important example of a gothic text that responds to concerns about American political leaders. In "Beaux Fest for the Wicked," men often appear like flawed Saints who direct power relations, and women compete for valuation from them.

Contemporary gothic literature provides an outlet from which to experience horror from anxieties on the outside rather than inside, and offers readers real physical sensations that speak from the American culture's ideologies concerning the practical and the real. Henry James, F. Scott Fitzgerald and Ernest Hemingway's realistic representations of experience contrast sharply with Stephan King and Joyce Carol Oates's gothic depictions of consciousness, though, in my opinion, are no more effective in representing the real. The popularity of the gothic offers a glimpse into the mind of the literary reader and its relationship to the properties of the aesthetics at play in the texts. Gothic conventions are good to depict stories that illustrate the suffering and guilt involved in the expiation of trauma, and offers a unique perspective into the conditions of what it is to be human in postmodern western civilization.

Marilyn Brock

September 2009

Contents

Seattle's Best Neighborhood
12

Sterling
44

From the Edge of the Ocean
76

Rim of the World
118

The AX
152

Half-Hour Nirvana
173

Beaux Fest for the Wicked
192

Saving Mona Lisa
223

Boulder
233

Kauaian Sunset
257

Seattle's Best Neighborhood

The cow's body reminded me of the dead cavities hung frozen on meat hooks in gangster films. Flies buzzed around; it wasn't decent, the fact that the carcass was not buried. The poor dead animal. This was a significant creature, this black bovine, slaughtered by some mysterious force we were here to awe while mustering the famous nonchalance our Seattle grunge was supposed to convey. We slackers, in flannel, even me, a Catholic schoolgirl, *Latina,* like my mother said, with smooth black hair parted on the side, held by a barrette; I dug the clip in again because my hair was falling forward while I stood over the body in heavy dark sneakers that flattened the police tape which had fallen off a nearby post—the bull was missing part of its throat. Apple smoked a clove and pulled her parka closer; Natasha stood a few feet behind us. We were escorted by my father, Julio Alvarez, and I watched him lean over the bull and inspect the wound. After hearing the rumors from other kids, Apple, Natasha, and I had begged our parents to take us to see the slaughtered animals out here by the lake. My dad was the one who gave in; the stories reminded him of tales about the vampire like Chupacabras he'd heard about when he was a child in Guadalajara. He no longer believed in the supernatural tales that colored his youth; he wanted to teach me to be a respectable woman, someone who knew a thing or two, and this meant to develop a disbelief in what was foolish.

Holding Julio's arm, I took in the surreal landscape: marshy, twilit--a single dead black bull, maybe three hundred pounds. He'd thought we wouldn't see any animal corpses but here was a black Angus stretched out in all his dead glory.

"Let's go back," Natasha muttered, glancing at the farmhouse up the road. "The farmer might come home and think we had something to do with it."

"It's Chupacabras," Apple sighed. I'd told her about my father's grisly childhood stories when we first started hearing about the dead animals just outside the city. I remembered exactly where and when I'd told my friends—it was in that cafe downtown where we all hung out after school and were shooed away half the time like we were scaring away the "serious" customers—sitting at that marble, sticky, coffee-splattered countertop. Natasha and Apple quietly listened, their elbows on the counter, chins resting on their palms, and we unanimously decided that we would have to go see for ourselves if the rumors were true.

After our investigative visit, Julio seemed troubled and during the hour drive back to Seattle, explained to us about a succession of mammalian diseases that could kill a bull dead on the spot.

"Vicious viruses, aren't they? Rip your throats right out," Natasha voiced what we all were thinking.

"I'm sure that was the work of a scavenger," he interjected.

I was sitting in the back with Apple and ventured, "Dad, tell us about the Chupacabras."

"Perla, you know it's folklore."

"People believed it in Guadalajara--even he did, as a little boy," I said to Apple and Natasha.

Apple was staring at me with glassy blue eyes, and I clutched her hand, remembering what the Mexicans did to thwart the Chupacabras attacks.

"Don't worry," I whispered through her thin blond hair so my dad couldn't hear. "My dad knows how to stop it. He's got a special kind of gun—a rifle that shoots Varmint Load."

"That's good for *you*," Natasha mumbled.

"I thought he didn't believe in it," Apple murmured.

"But we can pray about it, too. And tell the government. The government should help us," Natasha whispered back to me and Apple.

"Dad, what's our senator's address?" I asked just as he pulled into our driveway. I realized he was frustrated because he was letting me off before taking my friends home. Apparently tired of dealing with me, that's how he dealt with my mom—Julio stayed away when he could.

Inside, I went to the fridge for a Coke and I saw the Las Vegas 1993 calendar my dad had taped up on the door. He'd brought it home from work, I guess; he was a contractor, and had been hired to build some new hotels. It was a big year for everyone—I had started high school, my dad got his project, my mom was getting her best tan ever, and the new neighbors—before we'd heard about the dead animals my friends and I were always talking about those boys who'd just moved in down the street. They seemed to live alone, just a bunch of teenage kids, and my friends were spending a lot more time at my house than usual so we could spy and conjecture on what was going on behind their front door.

Natasha Caveretti and Apple Beechman had been my best friends since grade school, and since my name was Perla Alvarez, our classmates called us the ABC girls. We ruled the school, if you know what I mean: The girls tried to dress like us, the boys made up rumors about us... people liked to talk about us just because it was exciting when they just had boring little lives. We lived in Seattle's best neighborhood. Many of the kids went to private school, especially Catholic; I was one of the few on my block who went to public because my father went to public college in California and believed in the system. Dad had dreamed his whole childhood about coming to America and making a great life for himself and his family. At eighteen, he made arrangements to go to junior college in Calexico, a California border town where his uncle lived. From there he won a contest to design a memorial for murdered American Indians. I'm not sure if the judges initially realized that he wasn't American--the irony, you know, that's what Dad said about winning a contest to design an American memorial, but he had a special talent in understanding how to find the doors to the other side. He talked to me at bedtime about the quality of memories and how they were our only link to the dead. His blueprint depicted an obsidian bridge to be constructed in Sand Creek, Colorado, the site of a massacre that took place just after the Civil War, except that the design was never approved--probably because they finally realized he wasn't an American citizen, I don't know. In any case, the recognition looked good on his vita and he got into UCLA shortly after marrying my mother in San Diego, which gave him his citizenship. A smart man, yes, and I was just like him, he used to tell me, way back before high school, when he used to tuck me in at night.

But my father's dream was only realized on the surface. There were private wars that I grew up around, deep within our big house my father bought when his success as an architect grew. My mother and father didn't like each other much. She was an idle white woman, and when he was pissed my father called her stupid. She expected too much--I remember when they got the limo for their fourteenth anniversary, and my father accompanied my beautiful Cherokee babysitter home while Mom cried on the living room couch. Instead of comforting her, I waited outside for him to come back, and when he did, he talked to me on the porch, just loud enough so my mother could overhear. "Your mother was never poor. She has no idea what it was like for me in Mexico, working on the ranch in desert heat, taking care of my family. My dreams were all I had to occupy my mind. They were all that I had that belonged to me. Elise, she just expects everything. Nothing has meaning to her."

"I'm like you, Daddy," was what I said.

The limo was typical; my father got one for every big event, even when I started high school last fall, he rented one for the drive. I knew I'd get one for my quinceanera, my debut party that would happen once summer came; all my father's relatives from Mexico were supposed to be there, most of when I had never met before. My father's parents were still living outside Guadalajara, along with three brothers, raising livestock. He'd lost a twin sister when he was a boy, my mother said she was the victim of an unsolved murder out on the ranch, one early morning when she was out feeding the chickens, and my father found it difficult to keep in touch with a past that hurt him so badly. His family kept in touch by mail, but other than the Catholic traditions my father had raised me with, I had very little contact with anyone from his background. I was as American as my mother; in fact, I couldn't even communicate with my Mexican relatives—my father wouldn't let me learn to speak Spanish because he wanted me to be like our neighbors.

Julio taught me the faith he'd grown up with, but he'd stopped going to Mass when a priest wouldn't marry him and my mother in a church because she was Presbyterian. It was no big deal to me, except that I wished I could have tried communion and worn the white dresses on Tuesday nights. It's been since I was eight that my parents have had separate bedrooms, and I've wondered a few times if maybe Dad should have listened to the priest.

But anyway, let's get back to my friends.

Like I said, this was a new year, a big one, and I could feel the energy of excitement all around me. Seattle had this new feeling, wasn't anymore just a tired city in the Northwest that was the setting for that Tom Hanks and Meg Ryan movie that all Dad's Las Vegas employees referred to when he told them we lived there (we all sleep fine, thank you). The music seemed to penetrate everywhere around us, like it was in the air. Everyone on MTV was talking about Seattle, the grungy teenagers and their music: Nirvana, Soundgarden, Alice in Chains, the Screaming Trees, and uh, Nirvana, Nirvana, Nirvana. I wanted to try our coffee (Dad had outlawed caffeine in our house, on account of Mom's excitability but I knew where to get some) and hang out after school in record shops and cafes. There was a tension about having the teenagers take over the city; it brought Seattle attention but it threatened adults because it undermined the system, as Dad put it. Adults wanted the city to be known for its cosmopolitan culture, but the national media was showering all its attention on us flannel-wearing kids.

At first I thought it was probably suburbanite shop owners who loathed Seattle's new grunge image that started the rumors about the dead animals, just to scapegoat teenagers, like we were vampires, monsters, or something—ruining Seattle for the heck of it with our libertine abuses of freedom. As if we just had nothing better to do! When I relayed the stories from my father's childhood to Natasha and Apple, I remembered the manager staring at me, grimacing when I explained how the cows and sheep had their throats or bellies cut and their blood drained ("No communion grape juice there," I told them, "The real stuff. Disgusting"), just like the rumors we were hearing now about Seattle's livestock. The manager interjected, while filling another customer's cup, that he'd heard from a farmer that it was just a bunch of stoned teenagers doing the killing.

I'd heard of cow-tipping, sure--through the movies. So stupid, right? But I knew that killing Washington's livestock was not what teenagers did for fun. I retorted that the stories reminded me of the Chupacabras—a monster that was rumored to kill the animals on my grandparents ranch and others outside of Guadalajara. Of course, we were pushed away as usual. But that night at home when I ate dinner with my father in front of the TV, I told him my theory that the rumors that teenagers had done it were probably false, and rooted in the establishment's resentment toward kids because of the way the grunge movement had reinvented the city--and he was proud of me. He replied, "Monsters seem to show up when people are nervous." And then he agreed to take us to the site, because he wanted to eclipse any possibility that I might still believe in the supernatural, something I was supposed to leave behind in childhood.

But I wasn't ready to give in to my father's mundane world, and believing in a half-bat half-goat killer had its mystique. And talking about mystique—those teenage boys down the block had it all over. They lived in the very last house, the one next to the highway, lined on the other side by trees. I'd watched a lot of flannel-wearing teenagers going in and out of the house, and at times even heard music. They were older boys who might not care about a kid like me, but I knew pretty soon I was going to make an impression--I was just taking my time coming up with the right one.

So one Friday afternoon when my Dad had left for Nevada for three months and Mom was out back working on her tan (she lay out between our bird feeder and a big foil screen, and didn't worry about all the news on skin cancer; she smoked and drank Tab, too), I asked my friends to come over, and I shared a plan with them to meet the neighbors. I told them that my impression was going to be 'me with makeup, asking to borrow a garage tape'—of any kind. Seattle was brimming with awesome new music, garage bands were everywhere, and teenagers were passing homemade tapes all around. I imagined that these boys would have some good ones. Apple, Natasha and I put on powder-blue eye shadow and icy taupe lipstick; we used hot rollers and painted our nails blue. Then we got ready to knock on their door and I put on my best cool face.

"Hey," the tall one answered. I'd seen him smoking on the porch, his long legs stretched in front of him on the weeds that composed their lawn. His face was long, too—not as cute as I'd imagined from fifty feet away. But his skin was clear and he had on expensive flannel.

"Hey," Natasha said. I maintained my cool face, waiting to be asked in.

"Hey," Apple echoed.

I was getting annoyed by their apparent lack of conversational skills.

"What are you here for?" the boy asked.

"Got any garage tapes?" I replied. "I live down the block, by the way. You've got a lot of brothers, don't you? These are my friends, Natasha and Apple. I'm Perla."

"Yeah, okay. Want some coffee?"

We followed him down a long hallway strung with cowboy lassos, cowhides, sheriff stars, even a pair of chaps: netting landscaped the ceilings and guns and bottles hung at various points, making the net droop in places. I saw some dried out cacti in the nets as well.

"Nice ceiling," I said to him. I leaned on the breakfast bar while he pulled blue Styrofoam cups from the cabinet and placed one at a time under the tap of a metal canister. He handed me a steaming cup first before handing my friends the others. Then he lifted a small bin of powder creamer and raised his eyebrows at us.

"I'll take some," Apple replied. Beyond his head was a large, sparkling pool that looked overrun by long-legged teenagers. Eight or nine of them-- it was hard to see through the screen and the mesh netting that hung from the top of the porch outside the sliding-glass door.

"What's your name?" I asked. "Are those your brothers and sisters? You sure have a lot of them."

"Yeah."

"All of them?" Natasha said.

"Yeah."

"They can't all be related to you," Natasha pressed.

"In some way or another," he said.

"What's your name?" Apple repeated.

"Josh," he said. "Come out here." He walked ahead of us and opened the door. I took a sip of my coffee. My tongue burned, but I sipped more, savoring the acrid black flavor. Then I tried to drink it as fast as possible, even when it charred my throat, and was hoping to feel the effects of the caffeine.

"Hey," a skinny boy from the shallow end said. He had the same long jaw Josh had. He stretched out his arm and shook hands with each of us, making us wet. I was almost finished with my coffee and suddenly feeling wired. My legs tingled. I met more boys. Andy, Tim, Michael, Gabriel, Pete, Jonathon, Landon, Jude, and Willow—the girl.

"Where are your parents?" Apple asked Willow, who scowled in response.
She looked at Landon, her blond brother.

"My mom's in Texas," Landon said. "Willow's mom's coming out here tomorrow. I think his mom's coming tonight."

He gestured toward Josh.

"I thought you were siblings?" I asked.

"Different moms, remarriages," the girl said.

"You do all look alike." Apple squinted.

"You have the place to yourself?" I said.

"Yeah. In Texas it was just the same. My folks still have their ranch out there."

"My dad had a ranch—in Mexico," I replied.

"Does he still own it?" Josh asked.

"His family does."

"Have you been on a cattle drive?"

"No. I haven't been there."

"Those are cool," he said. "We're supposed to get another ranch here, but it hasn't happened yet. My dad's working on the deal."

"Get in," Landon replied.

I nodded--Natasha declined an invitation to swim, while Apple agreed. I wondered what the boys thought we were going to swim in.

"Swim in your underwear." Jonathon seemed to have read my mind, especially since he said that when looking at me. I thought of our makeup.

"Okay," Apple said and looked at Natasha and me. Natasha narrowed her eyes, but I was neutral--I'd heard of skinny-dipping. Underwear was close to bathing suits anyway and I disclosed this fact aloud.

Apple was already taking off her top by the time I finished my explanation, which was really meant for Natasha, who started to play with her fingernails. Landon led Apple in her pink polka-dot bra and panty set to the side of the pool that had the ladder. I tried to remember what underwear I had chosen. A navy set. Good choice. I wasn't going to be the prude that Natasha evidently was.

I slid off my jean skirt and tank top and looked down self-consciously as I stepped into the water. I ignored that Natasha's eyes were filling with tears, but her anxiety was warping my self confidence. Apple started making out with one of the boys….Landon, I think. Willow was watching them while holding onto the diving board, arms overhead. I began treading water when I felt a sharp kiss on the back of my neck; someone had lifted my hair aside before I'd noticed. I turned around and saw Gabriel standing in the water behind me. I reached over to the side ladder and got out.

"Maybe we should come back." I cleared my throat. "Can I have some more coffee?" I asked coolly of Josh.

"Spend the night," Andy said. "You can have all the coffee you want."

I looked at Natasha, who glared at me like she was blaming me for everything. I wasn't afraid of horny boys, it was not the big deal she was making it out to be.

"Maybe," I said and I got out of the pool with help from Andy, who gave me a Caribbean imprinted towel. Tortola Rum. These boys had traveled. He also handed me more coffee, which I gulped down. I picked up our dry clothes from the patio cement and motioned Apple to get out of the pool; I was beginning to feel embarrassed by her.

"Apple, come in with us," I said above the sounds of splashing and cars going by on the freeway. Apple quickly caught up with us, her panty set embarrassingly see-through until Josh mercifully handed her a towel.

"My God, Apple," I hissed. She didn't look at me. As I passed Josh, he pinched something metal into my palm hurting the bones in my hand. It was an unusually shiny new penny.

"What's this?" I asked as we followed him upstairs toward a room we could change in.

"There's an arcade up here," he told me.

He led us to a game room filled with pinball machines, air hockey, foosball, and the fake head of a Medusa-like fortuneteller inside a crystal ball.

"Creepy," Apple said.

"You can sleep in here if you want to spend the night. We have movies to watch downstairs."

"I'm leaving," Natasha said as soon as Josh had closed the door. "I feel like we're at a carnival sideshow."

"Natasha, I never knew you were such a deadbeat," Apple replied.

"I never knew you were such a slut," Natasha said back.

"We haven't even gotten the tape yet. It's not that bad," I said to Natasha.

"The whole pool thing freaked me out," Natasha pleaded. "It looks like they are the only ones who live here."

"I know," I replied. But I was intrigued. "What if they know something about the dead animals?"

"Why would they?" Apple replied.

"They think they're cowboys," Natasha mumbled.

"I want to see what they're all about," I said. "We can leave, but I'm going to come back later."

"I want to see Landon again," Apple said as she removed her wet underwear and put on her dry clothes without them. I followed suit, and we walked back downstairs, awkwardly holding our wet underthings. Everyone was still out back. I walked alone toward the glass door and waved at Josh.

"I'm going to come back," I called to him. I still held the penny inside my hand.

He nodded but did not smile. In fact, as I looked around the pool, filled with ten kids somehow linked by the same father, I was startled to see them all looking back, with not an expression among them. Willow was no exception, her face was in a shadow just underneath the diving board. She seemed to be keeping herself above water with no effort. A car on the highway startled me, and I walked back through the house to meet my friends by the front door.

"I feel wired from the coffee," I said as we left.

"I'm going this way." Natasha started walking separately from us, to the other side of the street, until she turned the corner and disappeared from view. I watched her leave, not looking at Apple. I noticed the wet underwear dripping on the sidewalk as we walked back to my house.

"I'm going to take a shower," I said to Apple. "Let me call you in a little bit."

Apple walked on toward home, a couple blocks away. I knew she'd be upset I didn't invite her back to the house with me, especially after how much I could tell Natasha had hurt her by calling her a slut. But I had a growing headache emanating from the back of my neck, and I felt the need to be alone. I went inside and put my underclothes in the washer before drawing a bath to relax in. I rinsed out my chlorinated hair and put my mouth under the running faucet for a moment, trying to rinse out a bitter aftertaste. My toes tingled and then I noticed the bathtub water looking slightly pink. I looked to see if I had been cut anywhere. I couldn't find anything wrong and I wasn't in pain, but the strange, bloodlike tint alarmed me so I got out. I wrapped up in a fluffy towel and went back to my room to lie down. I placed the penny on my dresser like it was a souvenir from the boys. In my memory scrapbook, I kept ticket stubs, pictures, a label from a bottle of sarsaparilla I'd drunk when we were on vacation in Vancouver, but this was my first keepsake penny.

My mother tried to coax me down to dinner a few hours later, but I told her I was sick because I'd tried drinking coffee, and she laughed because I'd done something we both knew Julio wouldn't like. I think she might have worried that I was sick, but she didn't voice this, and I avoided her until I heard her shut her bedroom door to go to sleep. I felt wide awake and compelled to go see the boys again—if anything, I just wanted to see these boys with their parents, inside eating dinner. I wanted to see them watching videos in their living room and putting their strange pennies into glass piggy banks. I wanted to see them compete at foosball and yell obscenities while I whispered with Willow about Kurt Cobain. I had a million questions about their strange lifestyle, but I suspected there had to be a normal explanation; I wanted to catch them doing something mundane, if only to restore my sense of order in the world.

When the dark deepened enough to start showing the stars, I put on a fresh outfit and headed out. My muscles ached from my neck clear down to my ankles, and I kept thinking that my hair felt wet, though I touched it on the way over several times and it had dried.

From the street, the house looked dark. I had seen that from my own window, but I was expecting to see movement as I got closer, like a flickering TV or a lamp from inside somewhere, yet it just looked vacant. I went to the front door and heard cars going by on the freeway from behind the backyard, and my eyes were still having difficulty adjusting to the darkness because the glinty silver of the door trim seemed to be bothering them. I rubbed my eyes, waited several minutes for someone to answer, and still heard nothing from inside. I walked around the side of the house and ducked through an opening in the wooden fence. I crept forward over knee-high weeds that lightly crunched underfoot. When the pool came into view I noticed how the water reflected the sky, only shinier, glossier, and then, as I approached the edge of the pool, I noticed the dark shapes that filled the bottom like an image of rain clouds. I looked overhead and saw clear blackness, matted with stars, then looked down again at the mottled shapes in the water, which no longer seemed to be reflecting anything from above.

Then the shapes came into view, bodies, nearly a dozen of them: wet clothes, floating dark hair, pale arms and faces exposed, eyes all closed. It was all the teenagers, asleep underwater, their limbs and heads clumped together, not floating but settled in deeply on the bottom of the pool. There were no air bubbles coming up, except for a tiny one that startled me. I looked, and it was Willow, her eyes suddenly opened, looking at me, daring. But she remained still, and all remained asleep, and I noticed my legs felt unstable underneath me. I was almost unable to move them, and then when I thought to run, and I started out of the backyard, I heard a thunderous splash of water that seconds later splashed all down my back.

Josh grabbed me by the arm, and I shrank against the wall of the house, at first shielding my eyes from his face.

"What?" he said.

"Let me go. I want to go home."

"There's something you need to see," he said.

"No, please, I don't want to," I pleaded. The others were soon coming up behind Josh, dripping trails of water along the cement. Willow was the last to get out of the pool, and she came closest to me.

"You have to come see," she replied--her soft voice made me feel less threatened; however, I knew I was not being given a choice when Josh closed the padlock on the side gate. I missed my dad, and I began to say my prayers, just loud enough that they could hear me while I waited on the side of the house as the group changed into dry clothes inside. Several minutes later, I heard the garage door open and a car pull out. Willow led me to the car. I was soon in the backseat, sitting on Gabriel's lap, while his brothers sat all around us. While we drove past my house, through the city, and out to the fields outside Seattle, I listened to Nirvana from the tape deck, and underneath the grinding guitars, I thought I heard the faint sounds of something scratching in the trunk.

It sounded like a mouse caught inside a kitchen cabinet, but the scratches were more insistent, begging--sounding like something scraping metal. I remembered those faces on the backs of mail flyers, missing girls that must have felt trapped like me before they died (and I always believed they were dead). This was it, I thought; and it hurt to swallow. But I felt strong, afraid but stoic; I was remembering my father's blueprints for the Sand Creek memorial and the way he'd imagined the transition of his sister's death—dying was just crossing a bridge to another place that was sure to come quickly.

The scratching sounds caused bile to back up in my throat, and the thought of my father, who'd be gutted and grief-stricken by my death, made me hate the boys with iron arrows that were poised inside my heart, ready to strike. Soon I recognized the field under the glossy black sky, and the marshes in the distance. I saw cows and sheep around a shed, fenced in by white picket—the scene where the slaughtered bull lay.

"Why are we here?" I asked over the Nirvana.

"It's nothing scary," Willow replied. When the car stopped, I was let out and pulled to the side by Willow. Landon went to the trunk and unlatched it, then backed up quickly. We all waited, watching the car, and then it jumped out in a flash, the creature, causing me to gasp and dig my nails into Landon's arm, and he punched my shoulder for it.

A mangy coyote sprang toward the field, its back covered in open wounds and patches of thin gray fur. Its mouth frothed with saliva, and it lunged at a shrieking sheep--I tried to call for someone to stop it, but I had no voice; I clutched my stomach when the monster lunged at the sheep's throat and clamped down, abruptly cutting off its pathetic cries. I thought to run, and I took off toward the shed, but Gabriel caught up and grabbed my arm, and then his mouth--it came down on my neck, a big, saliva-filled bite that hurt--and his hands ran down the length of my torso, mesmerizing me for a moment. I was afraid to move, lest he bite deeper, and also because, in some awfully transgressive, hateful way, it felt good.

I breathed deeply, and he sucked my neck: a hickey was all, I told myself, I'd gotten one before from Justin Livingston, just last month during the football game, underneath the stands where no one could see us, and afterwards I'd worn dark makeup and a turtleneck for three days --but this, this...I wasn't sure I would survive this kind of suction. He kissed my neck all over, then my hair, and then I grabbed his hands, which were reaching under my shirt, because I was sure I was gaining some control, he had to be turned on, and I remembered what my mother once told me when she was crying after a fight with Daddy, "There's nothing more powerful than a vulnerable woman."

And so I grabbed his hands and pulled them down to my underpants, so I could control him, and I looked at Gabriel and said, "I'll let you do this all the time if you take me home right now."

I hoped he was stupid; I was banking on it, for Julio, I had to save my Daddy, but he told me, "I just wanted to show you our pet. He's cool, isn't he?"

"Grotesque."

"We got him in Texas, where we moved from. He ate all our chickens."

"You should shoot him with Varmint Load."

"No way. He's scaring off McArthur, the guy who owns this ranch. My stepdad wants to buy it, but he won't let him, so we're stuck in the suburbs until he gets out of here. Says it's his family's place, but we'll get it. My stepdad owns some of the biggest ranches in Texas, but his business partners are up here, and he needs this one. We got to get this guy out."

I heard the diseased coyote howling and the sounds of the boys chasing it around the field with lassos.

"I need to go home. Please let me," I said.

"Don't say shit about the dog. I know you're cool, but you say anything and you're dust."

I pretended to zip my lips closed, and stared as honestly as possible into his blue eyes. I kept praying that they would take me home. Gabriel put his rough hand over my mouth until my lungs started freezing into ice; my hands clawed his shoulders, his muscles felt rock-hard under my fingernails, and I dug and dug and dug and dug until my arms went numb. I heard the moon in the sky echoing like a stinging bit of stardust in my ear; if I'd been hit by a meteorite, I wasn't sure. I was falling in some dream, hearing bad moon rising, letting go of my reality thread, losing it through numb fingers. Gabriel slung his arm around my bruised shoulder and led me back to the car when they'd corralled the coyote back into the trunk. I heard the monster scratching all the way back to the house, and when they let me out I released my very deepest screaming; but it was empty, rancid, nothing. I ran back home, the crystal moon following me, and opened the patio door with shaking hands, wracking myself nearly faint with sobs as rushed into my room. I remembered the penny on my dresser that I wanted to throw out of my window, and my neck was hurting from the hickeys, so I checked them in the mirror and I was scared how dark they were, nearly seeping through my paper skin. I covered them with a heavy knit scarf, got into bed, and pulled my blankets around me.

I dreamt the coyote attacked me, and the thought of the boys made me so nauseous that I knew it would be physically impossible to speak to anyone about what had happened or I'd throw up. I couldn't tell my mother, who I knew would ask me about my new scarf-wearing obsession. I couldn't tell Natasha and Apple, either—instead I'd tell them that I'd found all the boys making out in the pool, with Willow and everything, which would bother them enough to never ask about those neighbors again. Hopefully, McArthur would put up security cameras, so the boys would give up and move away. Maybe this happened, because for whatever reason, the house soon went up for sale, and they didn't bother me again.

And then my daddy came back from Las Vegas, and it was finally time for my quinceanera. I wore a billowy white dress, and held hands with my father in back of the limo on the way over, excited about my presentation to the world as a young woman.

He held my hand to help me out of the limo when we arrived at the church. He smelled drunk, maybe on wine, I don't know, but I squeezed his shoulder as he walked me in before his relatives. The hall was decorated with angels.

"Are you okay?" I asked him; he looked unsteady.

"Of course, Perla. I had a run-in with a creature, but everything's okay."

"What are you talking about?" I whispered, looking around at all the people there waiting for us.

"A coyote lurking in our backyard today--I had to shoot it with the rifle. It looked rabid. It was…definitely necessary. But you--you deserve a beautiful debut. I shouldn't be talking about this."

And that was the last I heard of the coyote; except for the howling—I couldn't get the sound of the howling of out of my head as I danced through the night.

Sterling

The parade passed by me; I met eyes with the girl holding the drum in the back, the last one from the USA band in Quebec City's International Summer Festival. She had light brown hair, a ponytail, had just gotten her braces off, I believed, because her smile was so cute, so there. I found myself humming; that's why she was looking at me--the little drummer girl. She was in red, white, and blue sequins, a racy outfit for a twelve-year-old. My sister Polly wore Vaseline on her teeth as a cheerleader in college, to remind her to smile. In this parade, Polly would have been out in front, like the majorette. I knew I wasn't the only one thinking this. I was afraid to turn and look at my father, to see his death; not physically, not really... but I knew, with a gripping sense of spiritual awareness that seemed to be deepening by the moment, when the finale of the Star-Spangled Banner echoed in my ear--while he hovered behind me watching the parade—his spirit was at long last, gone.

I wondered if Aunt Petra understood how the young girl would affect my father—she wasn't typically sensitive to the nature of others' experiences—if I tried to tell her about my recent spiritual awakening she would shake her head as soon as I started talking—judging, muttering, "No, no, no," for no reason except that she wasn't open to ideas that didn't originate from her own mind—I glanced at her with teary eyes and mixed feelings about what was sure to be a final release from a long struggle with my father's will to survive. I'd prayed and it had done no good, but it had brought me through the pain of seeing him on his way out; and I felt an odd sense of peace when I met Petra's eyes that told me with a squinty look of reticence that she didn't know how she was going to manage raising me and her own baby all by herself.

But I am starting at the ending; I should back up a bit. My father once had a different way of beginning things that went like this--clearing his throat, in a serious voice: *No one thought you'd be the one to survive.* (This is the story of my birth, a better place to start, I think). "Your mother died in childbirth," he'd explain. "The cord was wrapped around your throat, and the placenta blocked your exit--after hours of unsuccessful labor, you were delivered c-section and she passed away from a reaction to the antibiotics." The story helped me feel close to my mother, so my father told us every year on Christmas, when we most missed having a mother. My father wasn't religious, he was strictly scientific, but hearing the story of my mother's passing stirred something inside me, caused me to yearn for things I couldn't see, to wonder about the mysterious workings inside the beautiful Catholic cathedrals I'd walked past downtown. I told Polly that it made me feel spiritual; I could always swear when he talked about my mother that she was somewhere around us. Polly would listen sitting next to me on the double bed, wrapped in quilts, both our backs slunk against the brass headboard—I'd hug her bony frame, and the two of us would listen to how mother bloated with water, how her antibodies fought the Cipro just as my body, in an incubator a few doors down, was fighting the antibodies of her incompatible blood platelets. My father said while my mother was in labor with me, he didn't know which of us was going to live--and inside I thought, "But God chose me."

My family lived in Louisville when I was born, in a dark house near downtown—I call it dark because it was painted brown and looked ancient compared to the newer city buildings around us. It was a small remodeled farmhouse you might miss if you weren't looking for it because it was a few yards back from the street and half-obscured by an office building and trees. Someone in grade school said it was haunted, I think because it was built so many years before the houses around it and needed a paint job and a new porch swing (ours was broken and hung sideways) and could have used someone to trim the bushes.

At night, Polly would adjust the foil covered TV antenna for reruns of Little House on the Prairie, which we watched religiously ever since Father said, "We had no money, but we had love, like the Ingalls," after seeing an old episode together. Polly, who was five years older than me, became Mary, and I became Laura when we put on little skits from the show for our father after he'd come home from working in the stables at Churchill

Downs and had showered. He'd lean back on the big quilted bed and laugh when we'd call him Pa. Other times, early in the morning, we'd put on the our tape of the Macarena in our room, and burst in his room dancing in order to wake him up, usually having to stop halfway through because we couldn't stop laughing.

Oh God I told you what I would do and this doesn't make sense... You see I've prayed and prayed and Dad already lost my mother and I know this won't work this is the wrong way to do things

My mother's portrait hung above Dad's bed, like the Madonna, attached to the nail by a deep blue ribbon; it was a frame Polly had made for Father's Day and the picture, you see, my mother's head was tilted to the side-- one of those glamour shots, in black and white. Even when he had women over he never took it down; when he had girlfriends over, Polly and I used to leave and walk to Churchill Downs to see the horses. Henry, one of the groomers, was usually there on weekends, and he'd let us carefully pet the noses of some horses--if you talked sweetly enough to those powerful, silky creatures, they would let you stroke their heads. I loved Threshold Breeze; he'd let me kiss him on the nose, long neck bending forward, like I was his ten-year-old mistress. Polly loved the palest thoroughbred, named Lucky Dane. In May, during the Derby, we'd make any excuse to hang around in the parking lot and look at all the ladies hats in every configuration of feathers and flowers imaginable. Polly saved a peacock feather that dropped from a hat one afternoon, and I keep it here, on my dresser.

On other days, Polly and I walked along the edge of the Ohio River, sometimes watching the riverboat races. When one boat would win, the skipper would come out yelling, "River Supremacy!" holding big wide antlers to put on the riverboat's frontal mast. There was something about the river that felt spiritual to me; I mean, as close as I'd ever felt to spirituality when I'd been hearing about my mother. Polly told me that history was deep along the river, and I thought you could feel it like the fog, like ghosts of warriors whose spirits still fought in the fervent energy we saw in those riverboat races. But my favorite memories with Polly were when she took me to the Seelbach Hotel, just a short walk from the river; this spawned my fantasies of growing up to become a wealthy southern lady, like the women I saw checking in. The Seelbach's expansive architecture reminded me of the Catholic cathedrals I'd wondered about, and I told Polly when I grew up I was going to be the Christian sort of belle, the sort that was kind to her servants. Polly acted as my beau, and while we held hands walking down the gilded staircase between the first floor and the lobby, as often as the bellman would tolerate, I told her of how someday a staircase just like that would adorn my home, and the magnolia candles in the gift shop would be glittering in my parlor, and of course, those ornamental hats would be hanging on my rack, just inside the hand-carved front door. Polly had always figured in my dreams for what would become of my life. She was the cement between my father and me, the one who held our little family together and I've never been able to rearrange my thoughts around to fully envisioning a life where she isn't in it. Neither could my father.

If she lives I'll give all my money to an orphanage…all the money I ever earn If you give her to me I will never think a bad thought again

When the phone rings in the middle of the night it's never good, and I remember waking from comfortable sleep into a state of breathless disorientation. My father was on the phone in his bedroom, speaking more strongly than usual, like he was having trouble hearing the other person on the line. He cried out as if he'd been hit in the stomach, and I ran to his room. I saw him hang up the phone, but he wouldn't look at me while pulling bunches of clothes out of his paint-chipped drawers.

"What's happening?"

"I have to take a trip. Just a day or two." His voice was breaking into sobs.

"You have to tell me what happened."

"Go back to sleep," he barked and pulled his suitcase out of the closet. My mind was running to all corners of the earth, trying to figure what event would prompt such behavior. My sister was in Mexico, on spring break with her boyfriend, Gabriel, whom she'd met earlier in the year at the University of Louisville. I remembered the conversation when she'd asked my father's permission to go, and he hadn't been accepting.

"Where are you sleeping?" he'd asked two weeks earlier; Polly brought up the topic while we were all sitting on the front porch. She had her arm around me while we sat on the stairs; I was painting with nail polish a lucky horseshoe we'd found near the grandstands.

"A hotel. A nice one," she replied, looking at the starry design I was coloring in.

He sat behind us on the rocking chair, and started rocking back and forth, creaking the slats of the wooden porch.

"No," he replied.

"You can meet his dad," Polly pleaded, turning to look at him.

"I don't like him."

"Gabriel?"

"Either of them."

"What about what I think?"

"I said no," he replied, and went inside. Polly followed, working on him--I heard assurances about her safety, Gabriel's character. I heard doors slam and accusations about selfishness (both sides).

My father sounded younger than I'd ever thought of him, more like someone Polly's own age; someone who'd always planned for his daughter to take care of him since his wife had been taken. When Polly won him over with promises of a week's worth of his favorite meals, he agreed--which made me think he possessed the same combination of selfishness and irresistibility that a child had. He pouted before she left, and took to passing his sleepless nights on the living-room couch. His rocking on the porch grew increasingly urgent when my sister left for Mexico; as for me, I'd been envious after seeing the brochures she'd shown me; I imagined Polly swimming in azure water with dolphins and scores of giant lizards running along the shore. On the night before she left, she let me sleep with her on her double-sized mattress, the one with the brass headboard we used to share as children. I ached because she was leaving, and I wrapped my arms around her like I had when we were small. Her eighteen-year-old limbs had grown beautifully long and tanned, and she had the deep blond hair of my mother; no wonder boys were taking her away to exotic locations. She hugged me to sleep, and I wondered if a young man could ever make me feel as loved as much as she did.

My estranged Aunt Petra called me from her home in Quebec City the day after my father mysteriously left for Mexico, and in measured breaths told me, in her staunch middle-aged voice, "Gabriel and Polly were walking...."

My mind was already going, imagining them on a crowded Mexican street, Polly in her turquoise lace-up sandals, holding shopping bags with one hand and Gabriel's hand with the other.

"... down a main boulevard in Cozumel, and Polly was hit by a car."

I couldn't imagine what she had said, except that her voice sounded too loud and hurt my ears; I covered my mouth.

"Sterling?" I couldn't speak, and she continued, "Polly was waiting at the crosswalk, and a drunk driver cut the corner."

"Is she dead?" I murmured.

Petra paused, "She's on life-support. But it doesn't look good. Your father is going to stay with her for the time being. Gabriel has already flown home."

I hung up and curled on the couch--and that's when I started to pray... all sorts of things. What came to mind were phrases from movies, and children I'd overheard coming out of church when I'd been walking back from the river with Polly. The words came easily, because without my father to be strong I needed something else, and I just begged and begged, *Please save her, please, I'll never ask anything again, please don't let this happen, I believe in you, I do.*

Gabriel came over and hardly noticed the candles I'd lit around the living room, something I'd seen done in a movie when people prayed for their loved ones at church. He was broken apart, could only talk with his face covered, and related to me in severed sentences that'd Polly had been hit so hard that she'd lost her shoe; he saw it just there on the sidewalk amidst a chaotic mess of onlookers.

To be honest, I just wanted him to leave. He shouldn't have taken her anywhere; she was so special, so important. Isn't there a rule somewhere that men are supposed to walk on the outside of the sidewalk for this very reason? I let him hug me, but when he left I locked the door and begged harder.

Please God, not Polly.

And after that I began making my rounds, to every church I'd ever breezed past; I went to every cathedral in Louisville, entering through those heavy, musty doors and standing under brilliant painted, gilded, and stained glass windows for the first time. I breathed in the candle smoke and saved my very hardest prayers for the altars. I put my last quarters in offering jars and bruised my knees from kneeling. I stared into the eyes of every Jesus statue and every Madonna, asking that Polly might live. On Sunday, I prayed at the back of services called mass, and took communion; I imagined "Jesus's power" infusing her with life in the hospital while I swallowed the grape juice. I watched during an infant's baptism later that afternoon and asked that Polly might be able to be a mother someday; she had been like mine, you know, and she deserved a real chance. But no one seemed to be listening. There were no miracles to be had, no sudden news of her recovery, no waking up from the long sleep for my sister. In that Cozumel hospital, Polly eventually died.

When my father returned home from Mexico, he looked hollowed out; his facial bones appeared to stretch his skin like steel underneath a paper-thin canvas. He pulled his long-unused tools from a drawer in the kitchen and mended the swing out front late after dark. His eyes had a strange emptiness that made me fail to recognize him at times--especially in the middle of the night. Louisville was ghostly; when the river fog rolled in around our house, I found my father out on the porch swing sitting all the way to one side, like someone was out there with him. He didn't tell me that, but from inside, when I watched him through the living room window, and heard his quiet murmuring, and remembered his new, empty eyes, that's the thought that occurred to me—that he was talking to her. He was leaving, too-- turning toward the other side, toward Polly and my mother, the two young women he had truly loved in his self-serving, secular life--and I couldn't let him. Even if he'd rather be with them, which by the looks of him, I was sure of.

He stopping eating, and his color got worse. In the morning his skin nearly looked transparent, and in the sunlight, while he rocked on the porch, I could see the veins around his eyes. I started giving him glasses of water to make sure he didn't get dehydrated, but he wouldn't go to work, and we soon got a message on the machine that he was fired. My father was never a popular man, and we didn't hear much from the community; Henry stopped by once with flowers and food, but I was the only one who would eat. I called Petra because my father had never organized a funeral, and I told her about his condition; I asked why my father hadn't given me the news that Polly had been hit by a car and why he hadn't allowed me to come with him.

"He didn't have the strength, Sterling. He's needed women to prop him up all his life, starting with our mother. He's never developed coping skills, he's been busy sorting out his list of unmet needs--and I think this has just pushed him over the edge. Polly reminded him so much of your mother, you know."

"He's not using me as a prop; he's avoiding me," I replied. "Why doesn't he care about me?"

"I think he cares but he's overloaded."

But it was a paltry answer from a woman I found useless in offering me true comfort—and her explanation was no good excuse for my father's weakness.

"He can't take care of himself anymore," I replied, and Petra told me we needed to move in with her for the time being, and lamented a little bit about her financial situation, but offered to take care of managing our house if I agreed to drive him up.

Within a few days, Petra organized a packing service to move our belongings to Canada and I began driving my father up to her house on Isle D'Orleans with my learner's permit. Driving brought me the first flush of feeling I'd had since my sister's death two weeks earlier; I realized I'd been numb, and as I drove the old Dodge on the highways through Ohio and Pennsylvania and New York, my insides melted in pins and needles, like some feeling was thawing out. I had the maps spread out in the backseat, and hummed to music while my father remained silent, leaning against the window.

"You want to see Niagara Falls? We can pass by there. You've got to see it; it's supposed to be a miracle," I said.

"There are no miracles," he replied, slathering on his miserable, agnostic fate.

"I'm the driver; I get to choose."

Ordinarily, my father would have bristled, but he closed his eyes, and I felt a lump in my throat.

Don't leave yet.

Feelings of abandonment were pouring over me... a father should have a sense of duty... at the very least, the decency not to leave me alone so he can take off into some hellish emotional abyss. And I feared he might go to hell; after all, he didn't believe in God and lacked any kind of fatherly instinct to take care of me. I didn't want him to leave for many reasons—because I didn't want him to go to hell, because I didn't want to end up with Petra, because I didn't want to lose my only human connection to Polly and my mother, because I didn't want to be the last person in my family to survive—that was powerfully strange--and because I loved him, even if he didn't have it in him to love me in return.

In a few hours, I was jockeying the Dodge between cars paused along the street above the falls. The water roared and misted the air like a cold humidifier.

"Let's see it," I tugged at my father.

"You go," he said, irritated.

I got out and ran toward the water, even pushing through tourists who were sightseeing more casually than I was. I leaned on the rail over Horseshoe Falls and breathed in the mist. It did look like a miracle, like the very edge of the earth falling off. The sound of the rushing water silenced all my sadness a moment, just a moment, and then I had to get back to the car.

"You missed the ends of the earth," I said, starting the car again. He was looking toward the water. "We have to talk," I said. "My mom and Polly will be there when we get there, in heaven. There's no hurry," I told him, trying to encourage him to develop a sense of faith. I thought that heaven was a great motivator.

"There's no there. They're just dead, Sterling."

"I'm not sure I think that anymore. And maybe you don't either."

"I don't believe in heaven."

"You've been talking to Polly—or someone."

"I've been imagining talking to Polly, and your mother." He took my hand, which surprised me. His dramatic cheekbones and protruding upper jaw I still found unsettling, and unfamiliar.

"I'm afraid you want to die," I said, tears coming. A car honked behind us to move. "You can't do this to me. Don't you care about me?"

"Yes, I care about you." He turned his head to look outside again. I didn't believe him and I left him alone.

I drove thirteen more hours to Quebec City, with only a few stops, including Montreal, for food. My father finally agreed to eat some doughnuts from a Tim Horton's when I brought some back to the car. In the evening, we finally arrived at Petra's farmhouse on Isle d'Orleans, just across the bridge from Old Quebec. I hadn't seen her since her husband had up and left her and moved to New York City.

In the darkness, following my father's directions, I pulled into a driveway that sided a noisy chicken coop, and Petra emerged from her quaint dwelling in the process of wrapping a shawl around her stout body. She had you wrapped in her arms, and her broad smile made me feel happy we'd come. I slumped into a chair on the front porch, while father took his time getting out of the car. She told me the movers would be there in a few days, that sometimes Customs took their time with trucks coming to the island. She called for my father to come in, then led me to the guest room while they talked on the porch into the morning.

At first, I thought my father was improving. We liked the slow pace of life on Isle D'Orleans; he fed the chickens each morning and watched him at breakfast, making sure he had a bite or two. Petra bustled around as if business was usual, which caused me to feel less self-conscious about being in her home and eased the transition a bit, I think; she made us breakfast each morning and every evening I'd retire into a bed that she'd made up--I'd melt into it, amazed by the way it felt to be taken care of. She gave us leisurely tours around the pastoral island and we met some other nice neighbors who traveled with us across the bridge to see the Montmorency waterfall and the Chateau Frontenac in Old Quebec in the Dodge. The hotel looked like a castle, and the interior reminded me of the Seelbach a little bit, and of course, of Polly.

"Sterling," my father called after me when I left our small group, because I wanted to walk up an elaborate staircase in the lobby. I pushed back my shoulders like a Southern Belle, and remembered walking with Polly, imagining our futures; I wondered if God would have saved Polly if a person more worthy than I had been asking and I felt ashamed because I hadn't been raised knowing much about spirituality. The group caught up to me and Petra directed us out to the deck that overlooked the St. Lawrence River.

Petra's neighbors talked about the historic battles that caused Quebec's leaders to build a wall around the city.

"Is there a place to pray around here?" I interrupted off-topic.

My father looked up from his seat on the bench.

"Who are you asking?" he said.

"St. Anne's," Louise, Petra's neighbor, piped up, "just down the way from the falls. It's a very famous church for healing; there are crutches hung up inside the front door from people who claim to have been healed there."

"I want to go." I looked pleadingly at Petra, hoping for an ally.

"Of course," she said, and stopped to purchase maple beaver-tails for all of us to eat on the way over. My father passed his on to me.

"Praying?" he said in the car, pulling his jacket closer around him.

"I'm not talking to you," I crossed my arms and avoided his dismissive look. I passed his doughnut back over to him on the drive over, and he left it untouched on his thigh.

Louise directed me toward the cathedral and I saw it nearing toward us by the road; it was spectacular, all white and silver and pointing toward the sky. Petra, her neighbors, and my father stayed in the car while I left to go inside; immediately, I was awed by the awesome ceiling and the layers of crutches strung up all over the interior of the church's entrance.

God listens, I hoped—for some reason Polly had to leave but maybe my father could stay. I took a seat in back, closing my eyes near a row of lit candles that lined one wall, praying underneath spectacular gold and stained glass images overhead.

It was so hushed, quiet, and my horse came to mind—Threshold Breeze. Instead of praying, and a bit flustered in my awe, I remembered watching my black stallion galloping around the track with Polly at Churchill Downs.

"There you go, Sterling. Amazing," Polly had replied, holding the feather she'd saved from the Derby. His gait was powerful, wind-challenging, sending up gusts of dust whenever he passed us. I had imagining myself riding him that day, holding on to his mane and braving the wind that was sure to whip my face.

I tried to imagine this kind of strength for my father, and then I earnestly asked God,

Help my father find his way back. I don't want to be the last LeClair to survive. It's not

natural to be alone this soon. It's like I've become the dark horse outrunning everyone else in my family, winning the longest life. Surely this can't be the right plan.

My father was lost, unable to reinvent his life into anything livable after Polly's death; by rejecting his spirit, he was caught dead in his body, living life unconsciously. He needed to try and transform--reinvent himself in a way to fit in with a family that just included me. I looked at the statue of Madonna before I left, wondering if Polly was in some place like heaven, and went back to the car, sighing and slightly dizzy.

"You okay?" Petra asked me when I climbed back in the driver's seat. We waited a few moments for Petra's neighbors to return from a souvenir shop near the church. My father looked out the window at the river.

"Fine, yes," I said, and was glad when I saw Louise walking toward us so we could leave.

"What did you do?" Petra asked.

"I walked around the inside, I saw crutches on the inside of the church."

She was shaking her head and I stopped explaining. It was clear that while she'd taken care of me, she would never be able to understand the kind of dimension that spirituality had given my life—it was what was causing me to survive. Louise and her friend Edna asked to be dropped off, so I took them home and then Petra directed me to stop by a maple farm before we returned to the island. When I pulled the Dodge into the driveway, a half dozen husky puppies bounded up to greet us. I laughed and rubbed the back of the first one to get to me, while Father pulled himself out of the car, reluctantly, complaining about the cold weather. He rubbed his forearms with his hands and followed Petra and I inside into the crowded restaurant inside the maple farm.

"Ha! Everything maple—love this place," Petra exclaimed when we walked through the doors. The interior featured long tables with people eating plates of food, elbow to elbow. A sign "World Famous Maple Pancakes" was stretched over the stage, which featured a mariachi band and a handful of people dancing around them. Petra ordered three plates of pancakes at the grill while I found a few seats at the end of a table near the back. I folded my hands on top of the red-checked tablecloth and listened to the band. My father walked near me after milling around the maple items for sale near the cashier, and I patted the seat next to me when he walked over, holding plates of food Petra had passed to him.

"Avez-vous le plaisir d'erable?" I teased him in French.

"You mean this is maple? I was wondering what flavor," he joked, in spite of the maple-everywhere-signs. My shoulders melted—it was a sign of his old self—my Little House on the Prairie Pa.

Petra sat next to me with her plate and encouraged me to dance. I wanted to, if nothing else, to feel slightly less morose for one second. Then the band started playing the Macarena, and my mouth went dry.

"I'll go up there," I nodded quickly to Petra, and put down my fork and knife to join the burgeoning crowd at the front of restaurant. The lead singer sang the familiar lyrics that I quietly mouthed, at first not looking at my father, because I wanted to sing this for myself, to remember that I was still here, deserving to be happy for the mere fact that I was still alive, and possessed all the thousands of memories that only Polly and I had together. So I danced the Macarena for myself, not for Polly, and especially not for my father, who wasn't letting me forget that we'd been left for one damn second. It was intoxicating, the singing, the energetic vibe from the families dancing around me, the smiling and laughing among people and the euphoric feeling I got from the blend of the guitars. For several minutes I lost myself in that spin, thinking nothing, just being, and then I heard father yelling, his voice breaking in over the music, "Where are my keys!"

My eyes searched for our table; he was grabbing at the tablecloth, knocking over plates and bottles of syrup and water. Petra tried to grab hold of his shoulders but he ducked out of her grasp, yelling over and over again, "My keys? Someone stole my car keys!"

His voice was shrill like he'd just woken from sleep. The musicians stopped playing, the families stopped dancing--someone stepped on my foot, and before everyone could pause to stare at my hysterical father, rummaging across the tables and through his pockets, I lunged at the wall to turn off the light, hoping the plunge into darkness might preserve something of his dignity.

And then I ran to the back of the room, ignoring those who hollered out for someone to turn on the lights, and I found my father, who grabbed at my lapel and said, “Sterling, I can’t see--I’ve lost my keys.”

“I know. I know you did,” I was breathing quickly and got his hand so I could pull him out of the restaurant. Petra was close behind us, and I led him toward the Dodge, while he placed most of his weight on me with his arm slumped over my back.

The dogs ran over again but it irritated me this time. I helped my father into the car as quickly as possible, and reached in my pocket to put the key in the car.

“The keys,” I replied, holding them up briefly in front of my father, before putting them in the ignition.

No one said anything on the trip home and suddenly my father was asleep in the backseat.

Petra thought we should let him rest a few days, and then she planned to take him to her doctor.

"There's nothing wrong," I told her. "His spirit blew out when Polly died, and his body is just catching up."

"Nonsense," Petra muttered. "We'll get him back into routine in a couple days. He'll be fine." But the creases between her eyebrows forehead were tightly drawn.

"There's a fireworks show—a big festival coming up," she continued. "At the Montmorency waterfall, with a parade and bands and music, that might cheer him up."

"It might make him worse," I replied.

"He'll be fine," she repeated. "You won't lose them both."

But I knew she was wrong. When she called her doctor and got an appointment for the following week, I wondered if he'd make it that long. And I felt distant from him, not achingly sad and desperate like I had when Polly was dying, but remote, like I was dealing with the cast of a man I once knew, and had no one left in my immediate family; just myself.

My father took to sleeping on the porch at night, which bothered me, because I remembered when he used to go on the swing at night in Louisville right after Polly died; but on the weekend, he agreed to go with us to Montmorency and saw the fireworks show over the waterfall. Buses full of college students unloaded for the show, and Petra, my father and I got there early for a good seat in the booths.

And then that's when the drummer girl came out in the parade, looking like my sister, and he finally disappeared. I knew he was going to die that night, as his spirit had already left during the parade, and I kissed his forehead that night when he sat down on the porch, eyes blank as a cloudless blue sky. I said goodbye to no one, and no one responded. I said it for myself.

That night my father died in his sleep, lying on his side on the steps of the porch. The coroner, upon seeing his body stretched out on the wood like that, thought he had fallen but Petra told him that Father had taken to sleeping on the porch and that she supposed, glancing sideways at me, that his body had finally caught up with his spirit.

Inside, I was beginning to renew by the time the coroner came to take my father's body away—I was now an orphan in unfamiliar terrain, yet another version of Sterling LeClair. I looked at my sobbing aunt and held your little hand, it filled me with love despite all the sadness abound. You know, when my sister died, it was not immediate either; she died after a long hospital stay where she was kept alive; her sternum was crushed, but she was supported by a machine to keep her breathing. I remember trying to imagine her chest rising and falling, from the back of those churches, as if it would help somehow, to make sure she could breathe. I was wishing I could talk to her and I wondered if any part of her could hear me praying. I talked to God and took to finding cathedrals where I thought he would listen to me the most, the most beautiful cathedrals in Louisville, which I liked when they were empty, because I liked it most when we were alone, me and God, always clasping my hands and I hoping with everything in my being that he might save her… but it was too much to ask, you know, he never did.

I'm telling you this, baby cousin, because I want you to know how hard I tried for everyone. I took to taking care of you, because I knew there was nothing left for me to do for all whom I had loved. You're everything I have left, and you're perfect, sleeping in your little bed like this, wrapped up with me--your little fingers holding tight around my hand. I'm telling you when you sleep, because I know the wisest part of you hears me, and you won't forget. I wish you could tell me, little one, where you came from, before you were born to aunt Petra; and did you see God?

From the Edge of the Ocean

I lived six blocks from the graveyard. It was a compelling scene: magnificent lawns, elysian flowers in contrasting states of bloom, my majestic stone fountain. There were small paved roads that wound through green acres and the curbs were rounded, I would think for people who were too upset to drive well--or for the elderly, as so many of the funerals were attended by them. Only rarely did I get to see a funeral for someone young; rarely, but they were the best.

That thirteen-year-old's was memorable. A math whiz: I saw his picture passed around. He had short brown hair and a smattering of freckles--he wore small round glasses, reminded me of Harry Potter a little. I'm not sure why his parents buried him there, because he lived over in Silverton, and this graveyard was right on the bay; in fact, just beyond the casket we encircled was a tall Gothic fountain, and if you stood on the side of the basin you could see beyond the cliff to where the ocean began. I loved to watch from there that hazy line in the distance where the water and sky seemed to touch...especially at dusk, when that place seemed lit on fire.

Daniel was his name, and he died of lymphoma. Everyone was in black, and of course I was, too. His classmates read a poem they'd composed titled "The Boy Who Lived Forever," chronicling all the ways Daniel had changed their lives by his good deeds, and everyone was crying by the middle. I was touched by the line, "He knew just who needed help, and was always there. Daniel, we will remember how you cared." I knew I looked a few years older than thirteen, so I doubt they considered me a classmate. I imagined they thought I was the girl he'd always had the crush on, or maybe the babysitter's best friend. I wore a perfect black eyelet dress I'd made myself, and I'd pulled my white-blond hair straight back into a bun. I wore glasses that weren't real.

I thought about math and physics and all the subjects Daniel's classmates said he had liked. His parents had been so proud of him; they cried and held hands with his classmates after the poem was read. Daniel's younger brother held his mom's; a friend of Daniel's held mine. His hand was pudgy and sweaty, and I was startled by the feelings from him that pulsed up my arm. He seemed excited to be touching me, even through all his sadness. He really was sad; I could sense that, too.

And so the mother talked and then the brother talked and everyone was crying and then hugging and they put down so many beautiful flowers. I was crying myself. They put out hydrangeas, which are my favorite; I put a note in my diary that if I died I'd want hydrangeas. They did well by the ocean, and of course I wanted to be buried in this cemetery someday.

After everyone left I took a walk by the fountain and looked into the water I liked to use as a mirror. The glassy surface reflected the dark frames that encircled my eyes, making my face look a little smarter. I wondered what my new name could be, one that befitted my black dress and spectacles. I thought of Cathy from Wuthering Heights, but no, that was too common. Clarissa? What was a *smart* name? Marie. That famous scientist was named Marie.

So Marie I was, and I stayed by the fountain until darkness and watched my peach-red horizon and then did cartwheels on the damp grass. I smelled the fresh hydrangeas and then lay next to my favorite headstone, which had a pretty marble engraving I loved.

Amaryllis…you live in my heart forever. Edgar.

Amaryllis, I discovered, means eternal flower. I wondered about her underneath me, under layers of dirt and weed-roots and shellacked wood, maybe in some fancy dress. The reality of death didn't bother me, because I believed she lived on in some dismantled state, happier, I liked to imagine. I had just moved to California a few months before, all the way out from Ohio, and I knew no one, really. I lay on the earth and traced Edgar's name on the slab and imagined him an old hunchback, chain-smoking in his Sunset district apartment a few blocks away, ruined by Amaryllis's death thirty years or so before. He'd lost his faith when she died; in fact, the only thing he believed was forever was his loss, engraved in this stone, in cold cursive, under my eyes.

Edgar was young once, maybe wore glasses, and I imagined him blond, stately, possibly an equestrian. Amaryllis wore red dresses and made love to him on a golf course. Those were the memories he sat around thinking about while he smoked in his apartment, fifty-year-old moments.

I imagined Edgar thought about her funeral and how it had attracted hundreds, people who knew her when she sang in a pretty red dress at the fair, and that he thought about when he had left her during World War II, writing her letters every day, clutching her photograph in dim trenches while bombs exploded all around. “Amaryllis,” he’d prayed as he crouched under fire, thinking he would die any moment, “Amaryllis, you will live in my heart forever.” And he believed she could hear him, all the way from Germany to the edge of the California coast. But he survived and then when he’d returned never remembered to ask if she had heard him by some supernatural force.

I traced her name again, and I wanted to stay and finish the story, but I feared the groundskeeper would arrive at any moment; I'd only missed him by seconds the night before. I got up and dragged my fingers lightly across the water as I passed the fountain, then reluctantly turned and walked back home.

Father was eating in the living room, three beers by his plate, and I walked through to my room; I was still damp from the early-evening dew. I disliked the wetness seeping through my shoes from the graveyard grass and noticed the stains were beginning to build up on the carpet, a visible green.

"Daisy?" my father called as I closed my door.

Marie, Marie, Marie, I thought as I positioned my fake glasses higher on my nose and ignored his call; I could pretend I had my headphones on. He called again, sounding weary, and I put on music, but not before hearing my father's creaking footsteps approaching. I took off the fake glasses before he opened the door.

"Daisy, the school called. You've been nominated for Los Renombrados."

"They don't even know me," I replied. Los Renombrados was a year-end assembly program to honor those with good grades. Renombrados was a Spanish word meant to imply we were memorable students.

"They reviewed your transcripts from Ohio. Good work." My father was still somewhat sober, and I remembered that he was called a handsome man. My friends used to notice. He didn't look like a dad. He looked like a catalog guy.

"You should call Mother." I didn't look up, yet I sensed the door close.

I thought I would care more about Los Renombrados, but I felt nothing. I used to think that making something like that would cause people at my school to notice me for more than being the quiet girl who made all her own clothes. For the assembly, I'd have to give a quick speech. I knew where I could compile a lot of great quotes; the graveyard was filled with them.

"To the love of my life…we shall all remember…those who will always stay in our hearts….the best sons and daughters….loving wives and husbands....good- bye...amen...forever, everlasting love."

I checked for my father's copy of the Chronicle, which he usually left on my sewing table after he'd read it. The print was making the whitewashed wood a little gray, and I got up and rubbed on it for a second, then I browsed the funeral announcements.

"Loving sons and daughters, loving husbands and wives," I kept thinking absentmindedly. I looked out the window, missing that meaningful feeling I got at the graveyard, and how that might be intensified after dark. I imagined sparkling stars above the dewy grass and cold night air that felt like glass. I imagined Amaryllis in her red dress dancing with Edgar like they did in the '40s, circling the fountain gracefully. I imagined at night at the graveyard there was no time, just layers and layers of people's lives that were caught in various places, and that they returned to life in whatever age they were once happiest. The year was infinite.

I turned back to the paper and read about an upcoming funeral of a seventy-year-old nurse named Ann Richards. They printed a picture of her in her uniform and wrote that she had loved to sing; it was at two on Thursday.

Her hospital was just a few blocks away, so the next day I decided to see what I could find out about her. I kept her image in my mind: her dark, permed hair, her stocky frame, her compassionless gaze. She'd never married, a Florence Nightingale type, and I imagined she'd grown bitter over the years--too many patients she couldn't save, too many doctors without answers. She'd taken to church to help with the losses, help with her fears of becoming sick herself; and then one day she *had* gotten sick, and that's when the picture in the paper had been taken. She'd already known that a fight was futile, and her once greatest strength became her deepest hole; she had no compassion left for herself. She was nothing but angry that she had to die.

As I neared her former hospital I got chills down my arms, like I always did when I felt close to the dead, like they knew what I was doing, while no one walking past me saw me beyond my skin. As soon as I entered the building I saw a collage of her on the wall. There were pictures in all sizes, many with patients. She'd never had a chance to retire, never had a chance to marry; this was all of her.

I thought about Ann Richards while at school and then developed an outfit for her gathering that would help me blend in. The day of her funeral was even foggier than usual on the bay. I was freezing and resented the thin material I'd chosen for my black dress. I held hands with everyone in a circle around her casket. During the minister's tender speech, a woman at my side whispered to her friend, "She had such a sharp tongue," then added after a pause, "She used it on *me* once." A man sobbed openly, and the woman who'd criticized Ann, who was standing next to him, squeezed his hand intensely; I could see his fingertips turning white from the clench. The minister began with the Lord's Prayer, which everyone, except for the crying man, eventually joined, and then we all sang "Amazing Grace." I stood between two women in their sixties both in black chiffon, and the one squeezing the man's hand began to squeeze mine violently during more singing. My voice had never been too good, but I diligently tried to carry the tune and went along with most of the words okay. The minister had a handful of written statements from people too upset to speak. He read the notes: "She'd always been the mother hen," "always sang beautifully in choir," "always so generous." "And now she's dead," the minister then proclaimed with a decisive nod. I was guessing people might think I was someone from church, though no one acknowledged me, except that after the service the woman with the steel grip hugged me so tightly I almost burst into tears. The crush of her bones against mine made me wonder if I should have chosen this one; and later, as the mourners began to disperse, I saw her leave with the crying man, and I gathered that Ann Richards might have been treacherously close to the woman's husband.

I wanted to find another one to make me feel better, so I decided to stay longer, and at three I watched visitors congregate around a nearby grave, that of Louise Buckley, whose headstone bore the inscription *Forever in our hearts*. Her visitors were young, in their early thirties I suppose, which was me in fifteen years. For a second, I thought one woman looked like my mother, when she still looked reasonably good. I wondered if Father had ever called her, even just to tell her we were in San Francisco. It was embarrassing to admit, but I didn't think she wanted to know. She wanted to think her life started when she met Felix Taylor and moved across town. She wasn't strong enough to hold the various strands of her life together. Mother was the weakest person I'd ever known. Even I could put up with Father, and I wasn't strong. I wasn't.

By three-thirty, watching from a nearby grave, I saw that they were gathering to give Louise a birthday party. They ate cake and scattered long-stemmed roses. They were handsome people. Rich people. I thought the petal-laden cake looked really good.

A dark-haired guy in his late teens showed up halfway through. He sat behind everyone, not really talking, but no one seemed to bother with him. I would say he was cute, but that sounds so juvenile. But really, he was gorgeous in a roguish way.

He wore black, which was fitting, and I thought how well we matched. The sun began to dim into late afternoon, and the party eventually dispersed. I watched the succession of cars leave through the gates; one Beamer went over the rounded curb, just missing a flower arrangement. I looked back, and the boy was gone. Before I went home I watched the sunset while standing on the bordering wall of the fountain and then wished Amaryllis good-bye, if she could hear me.

At home, my father was reading Kerouac with the TV blasting. An empty whiskey bottle was on the floor by the couch, and I was careful not to knock it over as I walked by. He'd put the newspaper under my door, and I picked it up and hoped there were more pictures included that day. There was one, a Sheryl Kingsley, blond hair and a tight smile, who'd died of cancer three days before. Her eyeliner was outdated; she was fiftyish, young for cancer. Her heyday would have been the '60s, with that eyeliner and pale lipstick. She'd stayed in her heart a '60s girl, not accepting that the image in the mirror conflicted with the doe-eyed Jefferson Airplane lover, that time when she'd loved herself best.

Sheryl looked helpless in the picture, overtaken by cancer. I crinkled the page. My father made me angry when I couldn't concentrate on reading, all that loud TV. I screamed his name. No response. I felt my heart beat a minute, then calmly flattened the page. Sheryl Kingsley. I'd go see her.

I imagined a period dress with a geometric print and pale lipstick, my hair slightly teased at the crown, my eyes hidden behind tortoiseshell shades. I pictured the purchasing counter of the Salvation Army down the street, the collection of earrings, those gaudy clip-on flowers near the register. No, Sheryl wasn't that bad. I was being mean.

School tugged at my conscience, and I worried about the potential of my grades starting to slip. I'd worked too hard back in Ohio, though ever since we'd moved to California my nerves seemed raw and I couldn't concentrate; even the rose bouquets and hydrangeas sometimes weren't enough to calm my blood. I didn't like to think about Ohio and the friends I missed, and I still couldn't admit how angry I was at Mom for leaving us; I wasn't angry at her then, I was still angry at Father and the fact we'd moved all the way out to

San Francisco for an old girlfriend who wouldn't even return his calls.

My anger shifted to sadness when I saw the crowd gathered at Sheryl's funeral. I'd been wrong about her picture; I could usually tell better than that. People had loved her, cancer didn't get her easily, they were sobbing. Sheryl Kingsley must have been in business—her friends looked like they were competitive and in viscose suits. Maybe her picture was taken on a day when percentages had fallen.

I wasn't welcomed. The desperate sadness that caused the loved ones to hug you indiscriminately, to love you for being there for their loss, to give you endless credit up front, to believe you were there because you loved the dead one, too, was absent here. I was way too young and too '60s-looking. My tight frown and clip-on earrings were red herrings. I got the "Get out" sense, but grief overcomes anger. People couldn't bring themselves to say it.

But the strangest thing, beyond my misjudgment, was that I saw the dark-haired boy again, walking across the lawn. The minister was talking, and I was being eyed by the deceased's sister (I imagined--she had on dark glasses, but she seemed to be looking at me). I was feeling displaced, was beginning to question my whole funeralgoing interest, and then when I saw him, it was like that cliché that everything happens for a reason, in the way that I understood it at that time, like it had something to do with fate. He hadn't dressed to blend in like I always did; he looked the same as he had during the last funeral, yet it was unlikely that he knew both families. I looked him straight in the eyes and felt that prickly feeling up my arms when he looked back at me. He didn't shift his gaze. Finally, across the mourners, I mouthed to him, "Marry me."

It was a joke, except that I felt a flush of love graze my ribcage. He looked away quickly; I kept watching.

Finally the sister gave her last good-bye to Sheryl, and her wailing could be heard all the way to her car. When most of the others had filtered toward the dark caravan of limousines lined up against the rounded curbs, I approached the boy. He didn't bristle or walk away, but he said nothing.

"Why are you here again?" I asked.

"I can't believe you are. I knew you were an imposter. What are you doing?" he asked. "Obsessed with the dead?"

"No, I'm more interested in the living, actually."

"Why did you ask me to bury you?" he asked.

I laughed. "That's not what I said," I replied.

"Are you suicidal? Hanging around graveyards?"

"Far from it. I like all the flowers."

"Why don't you go home?"

"I could ask you the same thing." I was starting to get impatient. "I just moved here. I like it better here than at my house. My father's a recluse and always there. On disability."

"Is he an alkie?"

I thought he was going too far--I had expected romance, and this was completely uncomfortable. "What's your name?" I deflected.

"Dylan."

"OK, Dylan, well, I really just like being at the funerals. The sense of mystery--I wonder where these people have really gone, heaven, or just in the earth, you know. And what their lives were like, why it was it ended when it did, if there's any sense in that, a meaning. And they're all so sad, the people at the funerals. I feel for them. I want to care about them, if that makes any sense. It expands me, gets me out of the house, and, well, I *love* this fountain here." I pulled him over to my fountain and I checked my face in the water's reflection.

"What's *your* name?"

I told him Daisy, not a fake one. We talked longer, sitting on the edge of the fountain, and in my fingers I twirled a rose stem borrowed from Edith Washington's grave nearby. He told me he had attended a high school that neighbored mine and that he'd played football. His parents had known the people at the first funeral, but he'd come back to see if I'd be at another one because he knew I'd been an imposter.

"How did you know I didn't belong?" I asked.

"I knew everyone. No one knew you."

"Did they talk about it?" I'd always wondered if people ever reflected on me later on, if anyone ever noticed.

"No," he said. "I thought you were a ghost at first."

"Yeah?" I smiled.

"No," he replied. I started to ask him more about his family, and he interrupted, "Don't you think maybe it's rude to go to other people's funerals?"

I was hurt. "I hope not," I answered. "I want to blend in."

"Well, you don't. Not like you think you do."

"Yes, I do, Dylan."

"Well, I might come to some with you. Will you be here tomorrow?"

I asked why, and he explained that he was thinking a lot about death, and fearing it. He thought watching the funerals might help him lose his fear. "You can't be a guy and be afraid."

"You talk like you're still in the game," I said.

He squeezed my hand and walked toward the gate. I left my hand still a moment, thinking about how he felt; I wasn't used to touch all that much. The funeral hugs were always a little bit startling for me, the gripping of hands around the casket. Out of the context of strangers, with Dylan, my hand responded like it was falling asleep, though inside I felt like I was coming to life.

I reclined on the fountain, my back flat against the edge of the basin, and dangled my arm over the water. I let my fingertips graze the surface, noticing under my back how cold the concrete got as the sun set, even colder than the water that rippled around my hand. I remembered the groundskeeper again, closed my eyes to feel one last breeze, then made my way home.

As the sense of the graveyard faded behind me, and the six blocks between my little house and the expansive green passed, I could begin to hear my father's turntable, playing Sinatra, I think. No, playing Lawrence Welk.

I opened the door, expecting the alcohol smell that wafted forward. My father was waltzing around the living room, the end table kicked over, bottles splayed, his arms up as if holding an imaginary partner. He was humming. I tried to walk past him to the hallway when he quickly spun over and grabbed me into his waltz. I felt sick when he turned me toward the TV, afraid I was going to hit the coffee table, a bottle knocking into my left ankle. His hands held my wrists; his eyes were closed, humming whiskey like a fog around my cheek. He pushed me backward two steps, then pulled me forward. I was trying to unscrew my wrists from his grasp.

"You are nothing," I finally hissed. "You are *nothing*."

His grip faded a moment, and I began to hurry toward my room, when he suddenly pushed me against the wall, his hand at my throat.

"You speak to me with contempt?"

His voice was rough, like shedding scales. I wasn't scared. I wanted to answer, but my voicebox was beginning to feel bruised from his hand. I realized I'd hit my head against the wall, and the plaster felt hard against my back. I just wanted to go to my room. He looked like he couldn't focus. His bleary eyes were staring beyond my face.

"Where are you?" I managed to think but not say. I realized it was an odd thought. I still couldn't answer. Not out of fear, mind you. I just didn't care.

I imagined flicking him and him falling backwards. He let go and spun back into his waltz. I went into my room. Before I had closed the door I was already crying, which I hated. I thought it was just the squeezing of my nerves, the pressure of his palm on my neck, that brought about a teary reflex. I felt humiliated to cry because of it. On the bed, I buried my face in the crook of my elbow and hated my mother and hoped she was happy with Felix Taylor and hoped she'd have more babies with him so they could all grow up to hate her as much as I did.

The school called my dad the next day when I didn't go to the Los Renombrados assembly, I was busy finding the perfect spot at the graveyard to meet Dylan. I found a bench that, like the fountain, was high enough to see over the bluff, and I practiced conversations we could have and tried to imagine what he was doing throughout the day. By mid-morning I was losing hope he would show up again when I saw a hearse enter the gates. It was a funeral I hadn't anticipated, and I was wondering where it had been advertised when I saw the back window of the hearse open and a young hand waved to me. Squinting, I saw Dylan's face in sunglasses and smiling. I had to laugh. The car rolled to a stop by the fountain.

"What?" I whispered as I neared to back of the hearse.

"The driver is a friend of our housekeeper's. You can get in. Is this *death* enough for you?"

"It is *obvious*. Don't blow everything for me."

"It's creepy in here." He reached to pull my hand toward him. My hand got that falling-asleep feeling again, and I crept inside, lowering my head enough so as not to hit the ceiling. Dylan's legs were stretched out where the casket would be.

"You forgot the body," I said.

"We just threw it out on the way over."

"You could have strapped it to the top," I offered, smiling.

"Next time."

"Where did you get this?"

"He's a funeral director, like to help out," Dylan pointed to the driver.

"I'm not here to just screw around," I replied. "I just like the people, how they love their loved ones…" I was trying to find the words to explain.

"I think I like it here... it makes me feel more in the living," he cut in. "In real life I feel like I'm under a current, no one cares what I want, I always feel like my will is non-existent."

"That's what you feel," I said. "Tell me what you've never felt."

He was still touching my hand. "I don't know," he said.

"How much did you pay him to come along?" I wondered what the driver thought of our conversation.

"He just likes me," Dylan vaguely replied.

I glanced around. The grounds were empty. I knew of a funeral at noon, but that was still an hour away.

"There's another funeral; we have to stop," I told him. The groundskeeper was working around some graves near the bluff, and fortunately didn't seem to have noticed our fun with the hearse. Dylan instructed the driver to take the hearse back, and we watched from the bench as the Salinger party began to arrive. A casket was unloaded by the pallbearers and placed over the gravesite. A crowd of elderly people dressed in shades of gray and black faced a microphone set up by the minister. The fog began to roll in, causing people to pull at their clothes. No one was crying, and I was wondering what Dylan thought as he watched.

After the minister said the 23rd Psalm, a woman took the microphone and spoke of how wonderful Abbey had been. Dylan took my hand and edged us closer. I was worried we wouldn't blend in, there being two of us, and I hadn't studied anything about Abbey; I had only just learned her name by her friend's words at the microphone. My chest pounded as we inched closer. I reached for the dark glasses I wished I had on. I combed my free hand through my bangs.

"She managed the youth group with an open heart, loving those kids, giving them all her time," the speaker was saying.

“Amen,” a few chorused. I knew it was a church group, Baptist maybe.

The speaker stepped down and handed the mike to a long-haired teenage boy.

“Abbey was great,” he said in a deliberate tone. “And she wasn’t so uptight for a church lady. When she’d get pissed she’d give us the middle finger and all that. She didn’t take any crap from us. She was cool. And I’m sorry she died.”

There was silence. The boy sadly replaced the microphone, and Dylan squeezed my shoulder. I was afraid to look at him, nervous that someone might notice any asides between us, but I could feel Dylan looking at me, waiting for me to respond in some way. Someone in front of me coughed; another cleared her throat. And when there were no more responses, the minister stepped back up and finished with the Lord’s Prayer.

“That *boy*,” a woman gasped to her husband as the people began to disperse.

“Ridiculous. He should have been censored,” was her husband’s response.

I looked at Dylan. “We’re going to get in trouble. You should get the hearse and go.”

“That was awesome,” he said as we walked to the hearse. “I say let’s keep trying until someone notices.”

I was uncomfortable but nodded.

“I do feel better,” he said when he hugged me good-bye. “I see what you mean. Expanded.”

I watched him drive away and then went back near the fountain to remain as long as I dared. I watched the horizon transform into colors and darkness, and I wondered if Edgar was missing Amaryllis that very moment and if Dylan could possibly ever miss me and wondered about the creeping hope and fear that seemed to be melting around my lower back. I dangled my fingers in the basin and wished he would love me, that he would hug me like that again, and I imagined all the things he could say to me, that he’d never felt true love and now that he’d met me his life was filled with the idea that it really existed, and that even if we never saw each other again he would now always believe in it. He would hug me until my whole body felt like it was falling asleep, and then he would tell me that he *thinks* to me during the day, and that he wonders what I will consider about his decisions and that if we ever separated he would feel lost and empty because no one would understand him like I do and no one would really ever listen, at least not in the way that makes him feel heard. And then we would walk down by the ocean and we could talk of how we would travel to Germany and maybe Italy and find beautiful, ancient graveyards filled with people who had lived incredible lives and have amaryllis and roses and hydrangeas growing all over their graves.

I knew I needed to get home, and I planned to hurry into my room once there and pretend to be asleep if my father checked on me. I hoped he wouldn't be playing his music because that would mean he was lonely and upset, and I was relieved when I approached a quiet house. All night I hardly slept, and I thought of Dylan and traveling to Germany and maybe even living there and regretted having always taken Spanish. In the morning I went straight to the graveyard in a sundress.

What a warm day it was, so lovely, and I waited for him with an eagerness for company that I had never felt. I sat by Amaryllis's grave with my knees drawn up, and then all at once I saw him coming through the gates and the black and white polka dots on the dress of a girl walking beside him. Her dress was flouncy, and just above the hem her hand was wrapped around his. She had black hair and a Gothic pallor, with lipstick much too burgundy, and my eyes traveled across her hand and up his arm while avoiding his face, though from the corner of my eyes I saw his hair brushing against his jawline in the breeze. The girl was tall and not quite thin and not really beautiful, not in a physical sense, but I couldn't imagine her personality because she was walking there with him. I felt blocked and nauseous and Goddamn it. He never mentioned. His girlfriend.

There's this idea I used to have, something from a book I once read, that the wind could take your soul if it blew hard enough, and the breeze that ruffled her dress and his longish hair seemed to be violently ripping at the arteries around my heart. This acid wind also burned my eyes, and still I didn't look at him, not directly. When I breathed, it felt like the acid was going into my lungs, so I held my breath and asked mentally why he was pulling along the Girlfriend. I looked at her again. Her face didn't bother me, but her polka dots did, and those ruffles that ran along the neckline, which outlined the drape of a thin gold chain. She sat on the grass and looked at him while he sat next to her. She pulled his arm across her lap and gave me an ingenuous smile. I finally looked at him and he looked serious, unmoved…normal.

I stood on icepick legs.

"Have a seat," he offered. Same voice. I was hoping for a clone. Some explanation. His long-lost twin.

"How are you?" was all I could muster.

"This is my girlfriend. I've been telling her about you, how much fun you have here."

"This is so creepy. I can see the appeal," she replied.

"This is Angela," he continued.

"I'm getting over it," I said to them both.

"When are more funerals?" she asked.

"You can check the schedule in the paper," I said.

"Are you going to Sutherland's later?" Dylan asked.

"No," I replied.

"I wanted to go to one," she said.

"You wouldn't fit in," I said. "You have to blend."

She looked at him.

"Everyone is too overcome with grief to notice," Dylan replied.

"They might notice the both of you," I said.

"They didn't notice us," Dylan countered.

I liked that he called us an us and that made me sad. I started fighting my grief.

"It would definitely not work for three of us," I said.

"I don't have to go," Angela demurred.

I was silent, conscious of my frozen legs and that my homemade dress was blowing around them. I placed my hands on my thighs to stop it.

"Daisy's not going, I guess," Dylan said to her.

I said nothing. Lovebirds.

"Want to walk around with us?" he asked.

"I have to leave." Shuddering with indignation, I walked toward the fountain, and I made myself really mad by crying. I was far enough away by the time I started to wail that I was sure they couldn't hear me; I crouched behind the fountain so they'd think I left and crawled by some hydrangea. The blooms made deep impressions on my wet face as I lay there in the flower bed until darkness began to fall; the Sutherland funeral had long passed. I hoped they'd been thrown out and imagined a humiliating scene of that happening. I was angry that they could ruin my whole life here if they were obvious, which of course they would be.

I lay in the dusky light, tired from crying. On my left I could see Amaryllis's grave and a blond woman, wearing an ankle-grazing red dress, coming to visit her. She put flowers by the grave. I knew the dim light could conceal my bloated eyes, and so I approached her.

"Hi," I said softly. She turned, startled, and looked like a familiar daytime soap star.

"You scared me." She put her hand to her throat.

"Did you know Amaryllis?"

"She was my aunt. Who are you?" She was guarded, angry maybe.

"I have a relative buried here, but I wanted to meet someone who knew Amaryllis. I heard she was a wonderful person." I was exaggerating; I'd never heard anything about Amaryllis. In fact, this was the first time I'd ever seen anyone visit her. I'd imagined Edgar was too old and sick to leave his apartment.

"Who told you that?" she asked.

"Overheard it." I waved my hand vaguely. The woman's eyes softened, like she was taking pity on me.

"Very beautiful in her day," she replied.

"How is Edgar doing?" I asked.

She stood up and clutched her purse to her chest, looking around. "It's too cold out for you," she said. "You need to put a coat on."

She started toward her car, which was parked on the rounded curb, and I grabbed her arm.

"Please, what did she look like?" I didn't want to be alone. If I couldn't know Amaryllis, I wanted to know her niece.

"You shouldn't be out here, little girl." She excused herself by pulling away from me and walked toward her car. Who was a little girl? She drove away and I wondered why she'd chosen this day to visit. Amaryllis's birthday, anniversary or was this the day of the month she'd died?

Depressed, I thought of going home. A new dress was coming to me. I could already see it in the process of its creation, like Cinderella's ball dress being sewn by mice; mine would be red, like Amaryllis's niece's, but with a neckline that plunged navel deep. I went straight home to raid my closet, where I knew there was some red fabric, fabric I grabbed and ripped in half, pulling the material into two parts I could pattern into a gown. I was imagining the pattern as I threaded the machine in my room, mentally throwing beads around the neckline, no, pearls, no, bare. I kept pinning my fingers with the electric needle because I was going too fast, and my blood flow seemed to pulse with the tempo of the machine and was even spilling on the material, but it wasn't that noticeable. When I was done, in a frenzied mental instant that must have taken hours because the sky had become an obsidian black, I could hear my father singing Sinatra. Drunken singing, and I searched for my headphones and caught a glimpse of my face in the mirror. I looked upset and needed dark makeup.

So I made up my face while my father's crooning pulled out my nerves, making me hate him, though at that time it was easier to think of hating him for being a loser and even, for a moment, for losing my mother rather than hating myself for losing Dylan. I knew what I was doing. I wanted to smash the mirror, except I thought I looked pretty.

My father was in the process of passing out on the couch, whiskey bottle on the coffee table, turntable needle whistling on the edge of the record. His songs were now the vague hums and settlings of sleep. I walked back to the graveyard.

I knew I looked gorgeous. I could feel the cool air over my breasts and the exposed skin between them. The red material hung like a V between them, and my hips pulled slight horizontal lines across the skirt. As I entered the gate, I saw the groundskeeper, a small, long-faced man, sweeping up dead flowers on graves. He gazed at me in the darkness, looking shocked. Trying to look sexy, I watched him and undid a barrette that had pulled up one side of my hair. He didn't stop me from entering the gates, he said nothing, kept raking, but was stealing indirect glances in my direction.

I walked to the fountain and tried in vain to see my reflection; I imagined a flower in my hair to replace the barrette and looked for a large amaryllis among the graves, eventually finding one. I knew I had to see her grave, Amaryllis's, with my flower, with my dress. The polka dots were still gathering at the soft underneath of my mind, bothering me, and I breathed and stood in front of her headstone.

Amaryllis…you live in my heart forever. Edgar.

Her flowers looked beautiful in the darkness. I closed my eyes and rested my feet at the base of her grave, facing her headstone. I imagined Edgar, crying in San Francisco, old and no longer blond; old and no longer loved. The night was black like onyx, and I felt heady like I was dreaming, and I could imagine the way they danced in the '40s, over a golf course in a darkness like tonight's, like Fred and Ginger, with amaryllis in her hair. My hands shook beside my skirt, and when I raised my hands my imagination grew stronger, and it was like they were around me, waltzing, and I didn't want to open my eyes because I was afraid I wouldn't really see them. He was young now, handsome. A soldier maybe. About to go to war. God, they loved each other. The golf course bordered a fair, and I could feel the lights going up behind me. Small white Christmas lights that lined a Ferris wheel, going up and over, filled with happy families. A little girl was walking around with cotton candy, hair parted on the side with a big navy bow. She was in a sailor dress. Behind her up came a rollercoaster, dotted with more white lights. It was like a boardwalk; more lovers on the coaster, holding hands, a big band within earshot. Edgar and Amaryllis waltzing on the golf course, all the green filled not with graves but with grass and sand pits. They were in the darkness, enough removed from the fair that she could whisper to him that she wanted him there.

And so he made love to her on the ground, she in her red dancing dress. The flower fell out of her hair. I lay down on her grave, keeping my eyes closed, tears squeezing from under my lids because I wanted to be her so badly, and I called, "Edgar, I know what you feel. Love *me*, love *me*." I imagined he could hear me, old and hunchbacked in his apartment, and I made him cry too, because he could feel what I was reliving for him. And I lay on her grave and imagined myself Amaryllis, and Edgar rolling on her, on *me*, loving her thickly, feeling the grass underneath my skin, imagining the big band and the Ferris wheel music, hearing the distant children's laughter, smelling the flowers and sinking into ecstasy. Edgar knew all this, remembered all this from his San Francisco apartment; he could imagine it, see it like I could. There was only dead without her. I know this feeling.

I clutched the damp earth and breathed in her flower, but I still felt the polka dots gathering in my dress, and the screaming red material wasn't strong enough. I opened my eyes and felt the unbearable cold of the ocean-salt night air and the heartbreak that haunted the ground beneath me. I knew I had to go back to my alcohol-smelling home. There was nothing.

My bones felt stiff when I tried to rise, and I smoothed the red material of my dress. The graves seemed eerie, silent; the cement of the headstones seemed bright. The stars were obscured by fog that seemed to settle as night grew deeper. I sat hugging my knees for a moment; they were wet from the grass. My chest and neck seemed frozen.

I heard what sounded like the sudden splash of water coming from the ocean, and I got up to view the beach area by standing on the side of the fountain. In the darkness, on my tiptoes, I could see two bodies wading out among silver crests that momentarily appeared and then crumbled headlong onto the sand. I walked briskly from the fountain to the edge of the bluff that overlooked the narrow beach beneath. There were definitely two people walking into the ocean, past the red flag that warned of strong currents, past the do-not-swim sign. I narrowed my eyes a moment: Dylan and Angela, her flouncy dress dissolved under the water. I made my way down the embankment. My footsteps sank in the sand, and rhythmic waves cut the silence, slapping over one another. Empty beer bottles were littered around the shore, and I surmised they'd been drinking there while I was just above them, fantasizing the fair. I thought of calling, but I stopped myself. I was standing at the water's edge, hugging myself, and they were kissing just twenty feet from me. I thought I must be being punished, and I walked back up the bank and sat under a tree to watch them from the top of the cliff.

They were waist-deep in water; their faces looked ashen in the fog-dimmed moonlight. I thought Dylan looked at me for a moment, and his fingers flickered on his left hand, as if he was thinking something. His other hand gripped hers. They didn't move. Angela looked at him and then turned toward the horizon.

They kept drifting farther into the ocean. I knew they were drunk. I wasn't strong, but I was smart, and I knew what was going to happen. I kept watching as their laughter turned to struggle. I started to cry when her head went under and then Dylan's disappeared also. I felt myself trembling when they stopped coming up and the water looked like smooth black ice above what must have been their bodies beneath. I knew it would have been useless to try to find help because there was no one around except the groundskeeper, whom I hadn't seen in hours, and I took to sobbing when I looked at the moon; it seemed as if it, too, were swollen with tears.

I brushed dirt from my leaf-imprinted legs and walked back to the fountain. I kept reliving the way they'd slipped beneath the glassy sheen of the water, wondering where they were now, and if Dylan saw me there on the fountain. I imagined a headstone, one I could inscribe with "You will live in my heart forever," and a burial where I could take pictures of all the flowers and keep them in my room and look at them every day, maybe grow up and get a house nearby, keeping Father in a room in the garage, maybe call Mother, maybe to tell her the love of my life had died, and she'd come back, and I could take her to see Dylan, even visit him on my own, where he'd always be so loved by me. Though I wondered if I could have helped him, and I ached every time I remembered that I'd done nothing but watch him drown, and then that melting in my lower back would turn into a full-blown rage. I kept reminding myself that there was nothing that I could have done; I told myself that, that *no one* could have gotten there in time, and I kept remembering it that way, while I lay overnight on the fountain.

And so I made my way home again, dipping my fingers in the fountain before I left, dragging them lightly across the water, already missing Dylan, already missing Amaryllis, and as I neared the gates I kissed the headstone near the bench, the one of the eighteen-year-old boy who had died, and waved to the headstone of the nearby girl his same age, and wondered if I'd ever met him if he could have been my reason to believe that love existed somewhere for me.

Rim of the World

All my childhood I'd feared the sight of forest fires. We lived in a cabin above a deep ravine carved out by a stream that was flanked by evergreens. When I think of my formative years, I smell pine needles and eucalyptus and my mother's cooking. I hear the waterfall pounding from the edge of the mountain into the mouth of the hundred-foot ravine just beyond my backyard. I see the old wooden swing dangling mysteriously from a branch over the waterfall. I imagine the hours I spent across from that swing on another tree behind my house, the eucalyptus, my "thinking" tree. Its trunk grew horizontally, which made it perfect to lie back on, and it distantly faced the swing from across the divide. I was six or seven when I really got into deep thinking, and it was mainly inspired by that swing, which hung over a good twenty yards of thin air across the top of falls. I had different theories as to who had put it there, who had swung from it; I considered that it was a swing made hundreds of years earlier, and the ground beneath had since given way. I wondered if it'd been a site for executions; where fiendish murderers were swung until they fell into the ravine below (I was seven). The tree from which the swing depended clung precariously to the cliff's edge, so I imagined the swing was created and kept there by supernatural forces, that it was for the ghosts of children to ride on at night. What else could fearlessly swing from something that high? Then, as a teenager, I went through this period when I became too afraid to look at it.

My mother was a fearful lady. She had soft blond hair and small, kind eyes. She was shorter than other mothers, but her voice was sure and she was into safety. Two paths led from our backyard into the ravine: One, a definite trail, laced around the mountainside in a long, slow twist; the makeshift other was formed by rain and rushed you headlong through the trees. Every time I ventured down to the stream, I could hear my mother calling from the kitchen, "Take the Safe Way, Brett!"

My girlfriend thinks it makes perfect sense that I became a fireman; my mother conditioned me to be vigilant, wary that even a tiny kitchen fire could have led to the demise of our small Rockies town called the "Rim of the World." Linda's never understood the agony I face when I hear a call, the drop-dead fear that bellows louder in my head than the sirens. My legs feel weak, and I can hardly talk; I feel like my mother's son. I've always told myself that I'm not going to quit, though. I'm going to get over it, and the only way to do that is to keep up what I'm doing. The Chief says you don't know about courage until you've put your life on the line to save someone. I'll learn.

My girlfriend thinks it makes perfect sense, but it is my step-sister who drove me into it. My step-sister Elizabeth is my heart, the place where real courage comes from. That's what the anxiety is about, because Elizabeth's in there, and in real life she left me a long time ago, hollowing everything out except fear. I keep provoking myself like I'm trying to regain my sense of courage, or maybe I just want to find her during a call somewhere. She's been gone for eight years, disappeared at sixteen during an electrical storm, so I don't even know what she'd look like as an adult, though I've imagined it.

I've never stopped thinking about her. Her memories are grooved in my mind like the vinyl on my old records. I mentally play them like comforting tunes that keep my mind steady with what my heart feels like. If she died then I can stand that she's gone; I just can't stand the thought that she doesn't love me.

From my thinking tree I can see the waterfall that caused the ravine to form, and the sound of crashing water soothes me while I consider. I can imagine sometimes that she's at the top of the waterfall at night, among the ghost children, knowing the secrets of why the swing is there. If she's dead, she's practicing ethereal advantage and is even trying the swing out. I always wanted to as a child.

The bark seeps sap into my firehouse uniform. I'm supposed to go in right now, but something's always pulls me out here, day after day, to look at the waterfall. Maybe that's why I still live with my mom—I don't want to leave my old meeting-place with Elizabeth. I can hear Mom in the kitchen now, making spaghetti I would guess. The sound of water reminds me of my firehose spraying the buildings that went up last week. We don't get too many exciting calls, which is good, considering I have a hard time concentrating with Elizabeth filling so much of my mind these days, and the calls bother me so much. I think, and this is the real reason that I can't tell Mom or Linda, that I want to rescue Elizabeth. I am always hoping for that call that will be for her—even though I fear it. Maybe she's locked in an attic somewhere, held hostage by some depraved loner. Maybe she's had amnesia, and I'll find her with a different name, in some other town, married to someone my age.

I don't know which theory is true, but there is my fear that tells that she's alive and stays away because she never loved me, and there is my heart that whispers she is dead. The fear is stronger and always brings on her remembered voice. I can feel it filling the soft underneath of my brain.

"I love you," I make her say in my mind. She never said that. Then I remember a real time, a time with my mother in the kitchen. I was seventeen years old, sitting in the kitchen.

"She never cared about you," my mother said. It feels like it happened yesterday, as if I have no perspective, no gap in time or loss of immediacy.

"Don't you dare talk to me about her." My remembered voice is shrill, I sounded like my mother. I've grown out of that. I should have walked out of the room. Why argue? Except that I hated she was right, and I had to make her wrong. "You don't know anything about love. You just drive everyone away." It was the meanest thing I could think of. I was referring to her first two husbands. "I would divorce you, too." I wanted to be cruel. I wished she'd divorced Elizabeth's dad, so Elizabeth would be freed from the bonds of step-sisterhood and transferred into girlfriend domain. It dawned on me when I was seventeen that my mother was responsible for everything. If she'd gotten that damn divorce, Elizabeth wouldn't have been tormented by my love for her and eventually run off. And I'd have been with her, and I would not be left possessed by a ghost of some chick who lived with me, even when I have another girlfriend.

So Linda came to mind, and eased me back into the present. For a moment I remembered mother clutching her heart dramatically and trudging upstairs after I'd said that. I listened to the steps in my memory, feeling guilty both then and now, and freshly missing Elizabeth again. I mentally discarded Linda and thought of Elizabeth.

She was pretty. Especially naked. On my twin bed. When my mother was gone. She was my first, and I did it to her as much as she'd let me, which was a lot. She'd cry sometimes afterwards, and I'd hold her, appreciating her soft skin, wishing we could live together like that, imagining briefly our potential house, my mind wandering, knowing she was crying about the same thing, that my mom married her dad, and her dad left her, and she was in her stepbrother's arms. She told me the same story many times. I listened again and again, and even now, I am listening again, as I remember her telling me.

"Do you think we're going to hell?" Elizabeth said.

"There is no such thing," I'd assure her.

I said that to Elizabeth--so ironic, because I am this waiting hell now while I don't know what happened to her.

I remember one of the first days after she moved in with us. She was washing dishes, mine mainly. Eight years ago, she was standing by the sink in my kitchen, breathing with her mouth open slightly, like always.

Elizabeth's dress had been splashed by the water, and her long hair brushed the top of the basin. I watched it get wet, the blonde ends darkened with water. She looked at me, clear eyes rather blank.

"Brett, what are you doing?"

"I have nothing to do."

"Help me wash the dishes."

Her hands were soft in the bubbles. I touched them when she handed me a bowl under the water. I felt the tile against my stomach and her cotton dress against my side. She was about four inches shorter than me, tall for a girl.

"How is school?" I asked. I was fascinated with her like a rare species. I didn't want to ask too many questions. Still, they spilled out. "Do you like your classes? Who do you have this year?"

She was a grade behind me. She hadn't spoken too much. Her father seemed to be getting along with my mother fairly well. We were usually left alone in the house, strangers suddenly legally connected. I'd only met her once before she moved in.

It was like she read my thoughts. She said, "My father didn't tell me why we were moving here. My mother just died last year, and he pretty much stopped communicating with me. I didn't even know he had a new girlfriend."

"Well, now you have a brother." I tried to put a positive spin on things. My hand was outstretched under the water for another dish.

"He didn't tell me about you either."

She handed me the dish.

"Is it bad that I live here?" I asked, rather dramatically.

"It's your house."

"And is that *bad*?"

"I'm used to my old family. Just me and my parents. My friends."

"I'll introduce you around," I said.

I guess I wasn't terribly understanding, but I wasn't used to having a beautiful girl in the house. I was responding automatically, in a way she might find harmless enough to comfort her. I had only been used to living with my mother, a forty-three-year-old stay-at-home mom who was displaced when my father left in the middle of the night and never returned. She'd let her attorney find him, divorced him, and we never heard from him again. That's when my deep thoughts came in handy, when the swing swayed back and forth and pushed the emptiness into dark corners. I thought of executioners and ghost children and less of missing Dads.

Years later, however, I did think of beautiful girls. Beautiful long-haired blondes with wispy bodies and careful eyes like Elizabeth. It was around when my mother started going out more and returning with a lilt in her voice I hadn't heard before. She had this new outlook on life that seemed padded with optimism, telling me I looked chipper and other bizarre phrases. I knew she'd met somebody, and I was happy for her. I finally met Stephen after he asked Mom to marry him, and he moved in along with his beautiful daughter who was put into the room next to mine. She was thirteen. I was fifteen. I didn't know if I'd received the greatest blessing or the worst curse.

My friends thought it was the greatest blessing. It seemed I became more popular, as they all started hanging around, spending time in the bathroom I shared with her, as if the secret essence of girls could be found somewhere in her toiletries.

I left her alone as much as I could; she closed her door whenever she came home, wanting her space. I could smell her talcum powder on the robe she hung behind the shower, and I found myself more bothered than anything that was in there. I was fascinated, but still I was having my territory invaded. Greatest blessing or worst curse.... I pondered on the thinking tree.

One time, a few months after she moved in, I was deep into history homework on my bed when she opened the bathroom door to my room. She stood in her checkered skirt, way too '60s, looking hippie for the first time with her hair pulled back in a band. This was the '90s.

"Peace," I said.

"What are you reading?"

"School stuff. Come on in."

I heard my mother creak past in the hallway, walking to her room. Elizabeth's father wasn't in there. I imagined it meant they were starting to fight. I remembered the cycle with my father. Mother only went to bed first when my father was out smoking in the garage, mad.

"Do you think they're happy?" she asked me.

"Sure," I said, wondering if Elizabeth could possibly be happy living with me.

"I miss my mom," she said quietly.

"You seem like it."

"Sorry I don't talk to you more."

"You're a loner," I said. At school she ate by herself. Only my friends continued to say hi to her after it'd been generally agreed upon that she was an ice queen.

I thought she was just closed down. I thought about it a lot. People at school, in general, did not consider these types of things too deeply.

"I had a hard time accepting that I was going to live with a boy my age."

"I'm older."

"It's strange for me," she continued.

I knew she could feel my interest, and that was why she was uncomfortable. There was no good reason for her to be so guarded; I didn't do anything to her. I didn't snoop through her bathroom supplies like my friends did. I could see how she felt in the way she sat on the bed, like she was perched and would fly off if I flinched.

"It wouldn't be so strange if we hung out once in a while. You'd get to know me," I said.

"They might get divorced before that." She waved her hand toward the door.

"Nah," I said.

"I love you," she said. "I love you and I think you are hot."

I just made that up. Elizabeth never said that last line. It's interesting to imagine how differently that night would have gone if she had, because then I could have told her I did, and I could have slept with her.

But I didn't tell her I loved her then. She got up like a self-made princess but smiled at me the next day at school. Then we had lunch. I imagined we looked like a cute couple. My friends heckled that brother and sister were finally getting along.

"I love you, Elizabeth," I imagined telling her that day while I fantasized about making out with her on the field. I had spent so much time imagining scenarios, they were starting to seem like real memories.

I did tell her I loved her a few weeks later, however, for the first time. It was at the thinking tree, when I found her leaning against the slanted trunk, staring at the waterfall.

"Why do you think you love me?" she said, eyes passionless. I knew instantly that declared love--there was nothing less sexy.

I wasn't ready for that response, so I refused to reveal myself any further and walked back inside, stinging like I'd felt up a beehive.

Nowadays, I have become so accustomed to remembering her voice that it almost sounds like my own thoughts. When I watch TV, when I listen to the radio while driving, I can recall her voice commenting off and on…Her voice has a soft lilt that my mind exactly mimics.

I remember everything my stepsister loved. She loved ranch dressing; she loved our walks on the mossy rocks along the stream during the summers; she loved adding to my theories about the swing. Elizabeth thought the swing was part of an ancient community's ritual to sacrifice young women to malevolent natural forces in exchange for their peace and safety.

I toss my mother's keys off the table when I walk in after work, then kick them slightly after sitting down. Steam is accumulating above the Dutch oven on the stove; I get up to dump the spaghetti in the pot just as she walks in.

"Thank you," Mother says. Her feet are hurting today; I can tell by the way she walks, like she's stepping on stones. It isn't raining, which makes me worry that she is getting worse; her feet usually don't hurt in dry weather. Her hefty frame seems to be bearing down on the pads of her feet, as though her ankles are about to crush them underneath. Already, the crease around her ankles seems to be disappearing into a ring of falling down flesh. She picks her keys up off the floor and hangs them on a hook inside the pantry.

"Working today?"

She walks toward the stove, and I make room for her.

"Later." I lied; I wasn't going back in.

"Will you bring me some bread?"

"What kind?"

"Sourdough."

"I'll try."

"You're a sweetheart." She reaches out to pat my head, and I crook my neck to avoid contact.

"My neck hurts," I tell her, and walk upstairs to my room.

I am really going to see Linda. My girlfriend lives by the station; I can hear the sirens from her bedroom. She is hysterically in love with me. I think it is hysterical because I never have to do anything. Linda, in love with me at first sight: a year has passed and she still hasn't gotten over it.

While driving to her house, I remember the last time we had sex. It helps me relax a little. Elizabeth's voice drifts around in my consciousness while I remember getting on Linda.

I don't love you, Elizabeth says in my mind.

I know you do, I answer. Elizabeth really told me she didn't love me. I'm not remembering that wrong.

Really, I don't.

But I never believed her. Elizabeth seemed in love with me in a way that oozed through her skin and pulsed out her fingers but was left unsaid. She couldn't tell me because she was always standing inside this vacuum of taboo between us.

I used to beg, but she wouldn't admit it.

A fire engine passes my left, and I circle my Suburban up to the front of Linda's curved driveway. I go to the side door, as usual, where she is waiting for me behind the screen, and evidently crying.

"What's wrong?"

"I dreamt I killed myself."

She's been at work, because she's wearing makeup that is smeared all over her eyes. When she cries it makes her brown eyes look somewhat green and her lips look more bee-stung than normal. She's been home long enough to change. I hope her nurse's uniform isn't on the bed; I don't like the smell of burn victims that clings to the material.

"Why would that upset you?" I reply.

"Because all my patients were left alone."

"It was a dream."

“Dreams *mean* something. Maybe I can’t handle how much they need me. Maybe I think they are draining all the life out of me. Are you getting enough from me? How do you feel?”

“You’re alive.” I squeeze her shoulder.

“You’re laughing,” she sniffs.

“I’m not. Can I come inside?”

Linda opens the screen and steps aside. I find a place on the bed a few feet from the crumpled uniform. I lean back and surreptitiously nudge it off with my elbow while listening to her talk.

“Maybe I should do something else. You have no idea how much this takes out of me. So many of them die. And all that pain they’re in…sometimes I wish I could feel it for them, just to give them relief. It’s so hard to watch.”

“Come lie down,” I coax her, scooting toward the pillows. She pulls off her jeans and curls beside me in her T-shirt and underwear.

“Do you still love me? I love you so much,” she says.

“Yes, I love you.” My voice sounds deep inside my head.

Her room is so small. No wonder she loves me. There's nothing on the walls, just white, like she's is re-creating a sterile hospital room. She needs candles, something to add personality. She has a lot of records; I eye them, strewn next to her turntable. Mazzy Star, Better Than Ezra…nothing I listen to. We have nothing in common. My mother's cabin is so much better, even if I have no privacy. I wish I had my own entry. I should really just leave. I am making some money now.

"When does your shift start?"

"Tomorrow. For two days."

"You'll be in great shape."

"Yeah."

I feel like having sex, so I push my hand down the front of her underwear and kick off my jeans and roll over on her slender body. She pushes up the front of her T-shirt underneath me, so that the skin on our torsos touch, then pulls up my T-shirt haphazardly while I have sex with her. I begin to sweat, and our skin starts slicking, and it bothers me so I pull my shirt back down. I kiss her neck and her face and then finish with a gravelly sigh.

I am quiet, and she seems to fall asleep with her head in the crook of my neck. I reposition a pillow under my head and watch out the window. I hear the sirens plunge next door; I crunch the pillow around my head to cover my ears a few seconds. I wonder momentarily what the call is about, and then I hope my mother's feet aren't hurting her back at home. She just needs to lose weight is all. I want to help her. Maybe I could get Linda to talk to her; Mom might listen to a nurse.

My eyes search the sky outside, and I wonder about the dead and if Elizabeth is, if she now has some all seeing gaze penetrating straight through the clouds. I pull the blanket over to cover myself and lightly drum my fingers on Linda's black-haired head.

Elizabeth, I think.

A tear escapes down the side of my face, and I ashamedly wipe it away. The fact that I'm hollowed out by some chick who didn't give a crap about me is pathetic.

And she's gone anyway. What difference does it make if she loved me or not?

I know what I must have. It's post-traumatic stress disorder or something. Like what veterans come back with, and they still think they are in the war. Elizabeth has been gone eight years, and the more time passes, the deeper she gets in my mind, like some unsolvable puzzle forever unfolding. I'm twenty-five now and she is still sixteen to me, like she was when I last saw her, and she'd tell me my begging sounded like old tires screeching. My voice doesn't sound like old tires anymore, not when I am upset, not ever.

"Will you stay with my mom and help her lose weight?" I test if Linda is asleep.

"I don't think she will listen to me. She's so independent," Linda answers groggily.

"Just put the ideas in her head."

"Oh, the power of suggestion," Linda laughs. "When do you want me over to see her?"

"I have to work tomorrow."

I can tell this bugs her because she pulls the blanket up over her chest. She watches me a moment and then gets out of bed. Her tone is cheerful, nevertheless.

"No problem."

She probably sees it as a chance to bond as a family with mom and me. All she wants is to get out of working, marry a fireman and be in our house, even if my mother is living with us. Mother thinks Linda's nice, but she doesn't know how Linda tries to plaster herself onto me like wallpaper.

"Thanks."

I pull on my jeans and think about checking in at the station since I'm here next door. I won't. I'll go in tomorrow for my regular shift and stay two days. With Linda's help, mom will start to diet and her feet won't hurt her.

I tell her good-bye and leave. The Suburban outside overwhelms her driveway, and her house looks even more pathetic. I wonder again about the sirens I heard earlier. There are rarely fires in Rim of the World. People take care of their own, lead quiet lives. The calls are mainly false alarms in schools, sprinkler systems tripped off by accident in offices, people having chest pains. I had to *cross-train* as a paramedic in addition to my fire school. I liked the way that sounded, as if I am a professional twice over, but it was where I met Linda. She came in to show us how to treat burn victims, and I watched her slather bandages over a big fake dummy.

* * *

At six a.m. my alarm goes off; it's still dark out, and the cold's freezing my cheeks, nose, and ears while I put my gear in the back of the Suburban and take off for the station. There's a note in cursive, "sourdough," that's taped to my steering wheel because I forgot to bring the bread back. I shove it into the ashtray. I hope Linda makes an impression on Mom later.

I replay some of my arguments with Elizabeth on the way over—not out loud, just in my head. She tells me that our relationship was a sickness, and I explain that guilt is a matter of perspective, and if she will just hold on, our parents will someday divorce (or one will outlive the other) and we'll just be like any other couple. Marriage is hardly something sacred, I tell her, with all the divorces going around, not to mention all the unhappy couples, and I argue with her about how insignificant it is that her father married my mother.

Then I remember my argument with my mother about why Elizabeth left us a couple months after her dad broke up with my mother, ruining my life because I missed her so badly and we couldn't find her. My mom thought Elizabeth was dead, like that just happens to people—struck by lightning or something—disappear! I'm so angry when I pull up to the firehouse that I can hardly think. Why am I compelled to put myself through this day after day? I tell myself to remember to only listen to the radio in the car.

It's in your head that I loved you. I never did. It was all you, Elizabeth says.

I know she never said that. I am making up memories. This is just my fear talking, talking in her voice. Elizabeth said she didn't love me, but she never told me it was all me.

My heart's pounding, causing all my blood to go to my groin. Elizabeth made me mad a lot, but she also really turned me on.

I don't feel like dealing with the moods of the other firemen. Dave is already in his bunk, going back to sleep since there aren't any calls. No one else is there yet. I could have slept in later.

Feeling uncomfortably sex-driven, I get in my bunk and try to will down my erection by remembering when Elizabeth disappeared. That is always good for a mood change. I loved the hell out of her, and she freaking disappeared, like my love meant nothing. I would have loved her for twenty lifetimes, and she left when our parents' marriage was over, just when our life together could have been legitimate. And she's been completely gone ever since--I mean I can't track her anywhere, not even on the net. It seems like she's dead, but I haven't found out that information either. My mom heard some rumor from her lawyer that Elizabeth drowned in a boating accident seven years ago but could never get the information confirmed. The lawyer denied to me that he'd told my mom Elizabeth died, but I suspected by the way he wanted to get me off the phone that it was possible that Mom had regretting telling me about Elizabeth and had since asked that the lawyer deny the subject to me. When Mom told me this, back when I was seventeen, I threatened to leave Rim of the World and never speak to her again. I still think I should have left, in any case. Clearly, I'm haunted.

I roll over in my bunk because I hear some of the guys showing up outside and I don't want them to see what a weakling I can be, always wrestling with my issues. I just have post-traumatic stress disorder, and I can't say that to anybody. They would think I'm an idiot for developing something like that over a girl. No one even thought Elizabeth was that cute.

I try to calm myself by thinking about Linda.

I hear Nick talking to Aaron, and I pretend to be asleep for a few seconds. They are going to watch a movie in the lounge. It makes me feel like getting food, and I slide down the pole to the lounge downstairs. I avoid eye contact when I pass them, and make a big bowl of ravioli and coffee in the kitchen. I still don't feel like talking, so I eat alone in the dining room and watch the sun come up.

The sun is hardly breaking through, like a barely shining sliver through a blanket of heavy black fog. It looks like storms. I wonder when Linda is going to visit my mom. She told me she was coming in the morning and would bring some medical weight-loss pamphlets.

I know briefing is in a few minutes. I am hearing the other guys shuffle out of the lounge. I follow a few minutes later and sit in the back, say some hellos. There are six of us. The chief catches us up on the last few days. Storms today. Lots of lightning. Dry weather. Fire warnings. Nothing to worry about. A car has gone over the mountainside the night before. Slightly unusual. Victim was DOA. Car pulled up and impounded. Mr. Shelton suffered a heart attack again in his home. Three-car accident on Vine. Those of us on two-day shifts are not allowed to trade for a third day. I know that means me.

Around two, dispatch radios about a car accident. We pile in the truck, three of us in the back, Nick and Aaron on either side of me. Lieutenant Steve sits up front. My limbs are stiff with anxiety, and when Lieutenant sounds the siren, they go nearly flaccid. The garage doors roll up, and our truck cruises onto the street, making a path around pulled-over cars. There is no rain, but the sky is dark and lightning forks the horizon ahead of us. Nausea creeps into my throat, and I think of sex and Linda and Mom's spaghetti. I mentally promise to get Mom the bread. The siren begins to fade underneath my thoughts, and I think of Mazzy Star and how I should listen to the album. Linda saw them in concert two hours away in the city, and I didn't go with her.

We near the intersection, and I begin to feel my legs again. Lieutenant shuts off the siren, and I think I would rather die than go all the way down the mountain to see some stupid concert with Linda.

The accident is minor. Two women in a Toyota careened into a teenager in a Jetta. I stand next to the truck and unnecessarily open the panel where the Jaws of Life are stashed, trying to look useful. Aaron has a cigarette. The cops show up. We leave.

I watch a movie with the guys back at the firehouse, and then Linda calls. She tells me that she hates the storm and she's heard on the news that there were over fourteen thousand bolts in the last five hours. It's nearing four o'clock. I tell her it's just an electric storm, harmless, and to stay inside. Linda's an overreactress.

Linda says Mom didn't like the idea of the diet but was reading the pamphlets upstairs in bed.

Linda's cooking for her downstairs since Mom's feet are hurting. She's fed Mom's cat. I tell her thanks.

"Why do you have a gun here?" Linda asks.

"It was my stepdad's." I remember the shotgun in the pantry. It bugs me that she is looking through our house.

"Is it loaded?"

"Yep. Mom's paranoid. Single woman, you know."

"She's got you."

I hang up and watch the rest of the movie. My pager goes off. I check, and it's Linda again. I don't answer it. Then we hear dispatch. A house has been hit by lightning. Four alarm fire. Chief radios other districts for help. They range from thirty minutes to an hour away. We pull on our gear. I am shaking all the time, because it is my house.

They tell me to stay behind, but I say I'll follow in the Suburban. They get three in the backseat of the pumper, and Chief and Lieutenant ride in the front. The EMTs follow, and the second truck. We go all out. I know it's bad. I follow the pumper, winding through the idiots who can't even pull over properly. I think of Mom and then can't handle the anxiety, so my mind goes blank.

The sirens scream all the way up the hill, to the top of the ravine. You can hear the waterfall pounding behind the sight of the blazing flames. The top half of our house is engulfed. I have my hand on my pager. I pull my Suburban as close as I can get. Chief tells me to stay back. I run to the fire truck and look at the digital imaging of the house. I can see all the burning in infrared. It's mainly upstairs. A tree's been hit and fallen on the roof. I can see Mom's body upstairs. She's dead, it seems. Downstairs I see another figure. Pacing. Fuck. Linda. I'm numb, looking at thermostatic images of Mom and Linda. Another figure. Tiny. It's the cat. The cat's with Linda. Downstairs.

"We need to wait for backup," the chief warns. "We can't get through there."

Another part of the tree is burning in the front yard, nearing a gas line. There is no way Mom is alive, and there are only a few seconds to save Linda. I'm going in. Chief grabs my coat, and I shrug him off and get the hose to spray down my car and myself. I grab the fire extinguisher and release it all over the gas tank and engine. Before I get in, they try to grab me again, Nick and Dave, I think. I hit someone with my car door when I open it too quickly, and I slam on the gas, pitching the car through the fire. For a split second I'm engulfed in flames, all around the windows, and then I'm in the clear. I see my front door, put on my ventilator, and run through.

I have a strange realization that it is my house again once inside, as if I'd forgotten, and see the foyer above the stairs in flames. I look at the stairway and irrationally consider going up, but I know it's impossible to save Mother. There are only seconds here, so I go for Linda, who's in the kitchen, screaming. She's standing by the sink, the shotgun in her hand. There's blood all over the linoleum floor. And fur. She's shot the cat, and it splattered everywhere.

"I killed her cat," she says in a thin voice. "I didn't want it to get burned alive."

She's wild-eyed. I can't get near her because she puts the gun to her head.

"Linda, give me the gun," I shouted through the ventilator.

"We're going to die in here. I don't want to go through the pain."

"We're not; I'm going to get you out."

"*We're going to get burned alive*," she hisses. She shuts her eyes and I think of lunging before getting a better idea. I pushed aside the ventilator and replied, "What about the dog?"

"What?" she opens her eyes.

"What about the dog?"

"You don't have…." Her voice fades, and then she responds, lowering the gun, "When did you get a dog?"

I grab the gun the second it leaves range of her head, and she screams on and on. I throw the shotgun on the ground, fill the Dutch oven with water from the sink, and dump it on her a couple times. She keeps screaming hysterically. I grab her wrist and pull her out the back door, running as fast as I can with my hand gripping her arm. We run through a smattering of small fires and slide headlong into the ravine, down into the stream. There's an explosion, the gas pipe I realize, and pieces of the house rain down around us. I make it to the stream, pull her into it, and fall beside her.

Linda's fainted. I hear nothing for a moment except the pounding water, and then the sirens return. I look at the fire behind us, and then back over at the waterfall, where I see the swing.

It's going back and forth. I lie in the stream and the water runs all around me and my skin burns like hell and I don't know if Linda's alive. The swing's rocking back and forth and I look at the figure rocking in it, I look at her face and it's Elizabeth. Elizabeth's in the swing, still sixteen. She's looking right at me.

Her flesh is as real as I've ever seen and she seems to say something. She's too far away for me to hear her. But I see her eyes. She looks fine, not in pain the way I remember her. Beautiful, even more so. And then I realize Elizabeth has died; she died a long time ago.

Then I see Mom behind the swing, back on the land. Just like Mom, no risks. She looks at me a moment and smiles, like she's telling me she's fine. She turns and walks into the forest until she's too far away for me to see her anymore. I look back toward the swing, and it's still rocking, but Elizabeth isn't there.

I become aware of the water around me and my burning skin. My eyes are stinging; I roll over and try to rouse Linda. She's in shock, I think, passed out but not dead because her pulse is going. I take off my jacket, wrap her in it, and drag her out of the cold stream. She isn't burned too badly, but she's been scared almost to death; her skin's ash gray. I hear more sirens arriving, the next force. I close my eyes, and then I feel her.

She loves me, she tells me before she leaves again. *She loves me…she loves me… she loves me.*

And then she's gone, and I wait in the stream for someone to find me, with only the sounds of the waterfall and the endless sirens.

The AX

The seat is trembling, humming; I'm in a line, maybe four in front of me. I'm the white car, the one that looks like lightning on the track. I'm the female driver, the one Jessica will watch.

"Come on, honey, show them how it's done," the announcer hollers from the starting line; the car in front takes off. His jacket is patched with AX in red satin.

I forgot about the old lady, forty-five maybe; Jessica showed up after all. I watch her figure-eight around the last cones. He calls her honey, too, the autocross man. Honey--I think it's an Ohio thing.

Her car is blue, a Trans Am, which is rare in these races. She might win our round, and until last night, I was used to listening to her gloat about her speed in my Dad's living room at dinner, back when we were friends. She'd been engaged to him for two weeks, met him at a Burning Man festival after leaving her alcoholic, disability-insured first husband and Dad had just been laid off from his job at the tech company. I guess he told her about me under a Joshua tree between make-out sessions--not that I know him well. Honestly, I think that fact that he allowed me stay with him while I get over Brian was an emotional talent show for Jessica. He was never interested while my mom raised me, but I always wanted to know him and I was trying, watching him, I guess, as he courted his well-preserved intended. Jessica introduced me to autocrossing the week before, and I wanted to beat her and gloat over dinner; but I didn't win—well, I placed second, which is okay. Still, I'm jealous of her speed. Fifty-eight seconds is not bad for an amateur; my last time was sixty-three. But she's got about twenty-two years of driving practice on me, so I'm not to blame.

The cute guy with the wedding ring smiles and waves the checkered flag at the start line. Only three more and I'm up. Jessica is already back in her parking space, waiting for the next round. "You brought your grandma?" I hear an adolescent-looking driver joke to his friend as they walk by. I cringe on my dad's behalf. I'm feeling hate. Hey, she's fast, man, she's fast.

It's almost my turn. I drive to the line, straighten my helmet, look in the rearview mirror and fix my smudged eyeliner. My eyes look more blue. Brian would like that and I want him.

I try not to be self-conscious. The cute guy is smiling and motioning for me to roll my window down. I do and look over, listening above the sound of my engine.

"Try doing it in third." He holds up three fingers.

"That's not enough power."

"Otherwise you're killing your engine."

I don't believe this; I placed high last week in second, and it was my very first race. Sharp instincts, you know. Natural talent. I put it in second and floor the pedal when he drops the flag. The AX man is yelling, 'Look at her go!' but all I see is the road, the turn, the road, the orange of the cones, thoughts behind me, everything ahead, the speed, the freedom, my foot to the floor, the squealing of brakes around the corner, the thump of a cone under me, I envision soft plastic bending, making the next turn, I'm too slow now, the thought of the cone softened my drive, and I'm pulling in, let down. I don't want to look. Sixty-eight seconds. I drive back to my designated space, waiting for the next heat, embarrassed. I know Jessica is watching.

With my sweaty head to the steering wheel, I close my eyes. I have twenty minutes to wait. Eighteen cars in each heat. I can't beat the Porsches and Corvettes and Beamers this time. I can't even beat my dad's old lady. I'm in a Honda. A Prelude, mind you, but a Honda nonetheless.

Under my closed lids is the image of my father's living room, where I'm staying until I find a place of my own. Last night was such hell; it's hard to keep trying to avoid thinking about it. Waiting for my boyfriend (ex, I guess) to call….he never did. I lived with Brian, and we broke up. It wasn't sudden. Our relationship was a slow death I didn't want to see. I act like it was sudden, just so people will feel sorry for me. Friends care less if you are aware.

"What a dick" is what I want to keep hearing from everybody. I don't know why, considering he was very polite about the whole thing. He was perfect, actually. Always says the right thing, so graceful, so that no one can ever respond badly to anything he says or does; there was not a glass thrown, nor a slapped face. I had to take it well, considering I was listening to his well-mannered tone, which always kept me hemmed. He loved me but wasn't in love with me. And for him to deliberately say that meant I had to move out.

I showed my tears to Dad, not Brian. Jessica dropped my dad off to help me pack all of my stuff into my car, and we drove, me and my dad, three blocks down to his apartment, where Jessica had recently moved in. In a month, in a quiet ceremony planned in Cleveland, she would have become his sixth wife. With a teary face, I listened to my dad talk excitedly about her the whole three blocks; my numbed mind considered that my car was so overloaded I could hear the shocks grinding down. I even thought the tires might blow. My dad is over two hundred pounds, so he was half the reason the car was dying. I was dying, too, from something like thirst. I also seemed to have no clear recollection of where Dad lived, even though Brian and I had walked over there a couple times since we'd moved to northern Ohio for college, because I was hoping to become closer to Dad. I guess I had never actually driven the route, so it seemed surreal.

Dad helped me unpack and didn't ask too many questions, which was good. He still talked up Ohio, which had originally prompted me to convince Brian to leave Miami to be up here in the first place. And he gave some so-called dime-store philosophy (Mom had called him the dime-store philosopher) that made sense to me. When I hastily threw out Brian's UFO etching, the complicated one he'd created for me, Dad mysteriously told me that relationships were entrapments. I could have asked him to explain further, but I liked the way it sounded and wanted to keep the feeling I'd gotten from hearing it. It made me feel released.

So last night I made a bed on the floor even though Dad has a couch, because he and his fiancée were sitting on it and I didn't want to ask them to move (and who knows what goes on on the couch, anyway). Sheets on the floor were fine; I had my pillows from home, but I missed Brian's comfortable frame from when he used to sleep next to me. I remembered his deep breathing during the night, and I buried my face in the pillow until my mind was blank of him, because my throat was feeling full of broken glass. I had isolated myself because I was taking a hiatus from contact with our mutual friends (which was everyone I knew in Ohio). By my head I had a package of Nutter Butters from the AM/PM next door to Dad's complex. Really I was fine.

Dad and Jessica watched some game show. I lay behind them on the floor, eating cookies, and listened vaguely to the tinkling bell sounds from the show and wondered how the hell I ended up here at the base of a couch like this. I had little desire to return to college; it had been Brian's life I had been living out. And I had no idea how I was going to get back on track. It wasn't as if there was much of a future in autocross, which was the only thing I seemed to have natural talent for. I was ruining my car anyway; as it was, my car was still packed with my stuff and it wasn't good for the struts to keep driving it around like that.

Finally, past midnight, Dad and Jessica went to bed. Someone flicked off the TV, and for the first time, the bedroom door closed, I noticed the stars through the window. I watched them twinkle quietly and contemplated walking outside and seeing how bright they were, but worried it'd be too cold. The bedroom door opened again, and Jessica's steps crept into the living room. Suddenly she was at the foot of my makeshift bed.

"Samantha," she whispered. She bent to her knees and brushed my bangs out of my face. I watched her middle-aged face, which was new to me, since I was mostly used to Glenda, Dad's third wife (and the only one I'd gotten to know—I never even met his fifth). Jessica looked tender, glossy, maybe even a little bit drunk.

"I've had fantasies of making love to you," she replied. Her hand on my forehead felt like ice. I tasted the flavor of cookies in my mouth.

"I'm not gay."

"There's always a first time."

"I don't want to try." I felt her hand on my forehead and warmth reached into me; the deep well of sadness that had me content to be on the floor flooded into my throat, and before I knew it, I was accepting her mouth on mine.

So exotic, kissing Jessica felt like smothering myself in abyss. I wasn't gay--her female body confronted my sexuality like an angry bull, it wasn't seductively mysterious like a male's, but I succumbed, and let her feel under my nightgown like a wicked witch.

"Please," I mustered the will to pull away, needing a release from her strange comfort. Though it was dark, I think she could see my eyes, sad like those velvet paintings of forlorn kittens that were always on sale near the register at the AM/ PM because she replied, "I'm sorry," and crept back into the bedroom. The door shut after a long creak.

I finally exhaled and put the cookies under my pillow so no one would take any without my permission. I went outside, dressed only in my nightgown, and sat in my car, knocking my elbow on the framed prints that were jabbing between the bucket seats. I put my head on the steering wheel until my face became numb. At dawn, sleepless, I went back inside.

Later in the morning, Dad helped unpack my things from the car, while Jessica behaved as normally as could be expected. By nine I was moved into Dad's apartment and sick from fatigue and anger. I didn't tell him what happened and didn't know if I should. Dad and Jessica seemed wired after coffee. They went out to breakfast, and I tried to sleep at the base of the couch.

I woke from a half-lucid dream of Jessica brushing back my bangs again. That was enough to confuse me out of sleep. I found I was still craving cookies and water, so I went over to AM/PM and bought Oreos and Evian.

Halfway through my water bottle, I was at the entrance of my father's complex when I saw all the furniture on the lawn. I saw Jessica's artwork, her easel, her figurines, and her clothes in loose piles all over the grass. Jessica's Trans Am was next to mine, mostly filled with her stuff, which Dad had apparently been furiously packing. He was walking back to the car, with Jessica's cat under one arm, and placed it on the hood. The cat attempted to jump off, and my Dad caught it and put it more firmly on the hood, barking, "Stay!"

As soon as he stalked back toward the apartment, the cat leapt off and ran under some nearby bushes. Dad came out with another armload of stuff and threw it into her backseat.

"Why are you doing this?" I said.

"It's time for Jessica to move out." He was already ambling back toward the apartment, avoiding my eyes.

"Where is she?"

"At a neighbor's. We had a fight."

"Yeah, I would assume." I got into my Prelude and watched Dad, load after load, hurling all of Jessica's stuff into her car. His mood was impenetrably mean and I worried Jessica had told him about her so-called "fantasies."

Then I saw Jessica approach from the other side of the complex, and her tear-streaked face fall in horror when she saw what was happening to her stuff. When Dad saw her coming, he ran inside and locked her out. She pounded furiously on the door, screaming his name. I locked my car doors when Jessica turned back toward the parking lot.

"Your dad's a son of a bitch!" Jessica yelled as she passed. She punched her windshield and then bent over the hood, crying in earnest. Minutes later the police showed up. I guessed by their timing that a neighbor must have called them the minute they saw Dad streaming items outside the apartment, shouting insults.

Jessica followed the police to the door, and I rolled down my window so I could hear Dad explain that she was not on the lease and he was throwing her out. He didn't explain their disagreement, and amid protests from Jessica, the police told her to leave the property. Jessica sobbed concerns over her cat as she got in her car and left. One policeman asked my father who was "the girl parked out in the vehicle," and my father waved at me to come back inside.

"This is my daughter," he explained as I approached.

The two men filled out a report and shook hands with my father. I handed Dad the rest of the Oreos, which he asked to share when he saw them in my hand.

"Thanks," he replied.

"I can't believe you threw her out like that," I said. It seemed clear Dad knew something about Jessica's actions the night before, but I was afraid to bring it up. I knew that I needed to find another place, but I had no idea where to begin my life again. Rather desperately, I remembered the night stars, Brian's UFO drawing, and sleeplessly considered a job involved with astronomy.

"I don't feel like talking right now." He sighed and walked into the bedroom, closing the door behind him.

I wanted desperately to get to the race that was due to start in less than an hour, even if I had to confront Jessica, should she attend. I had a momentary concern about Jessica coming back and torching everything, yet after what I'd just seen, I wondered if my father was the "torture" instead. All the women he'd failed miserably with... what would they say about him? My mom rarely spoke about the past, so Dad as my father was some formless memory. I thought by staying with him he might show me some lost clue about who I was, if Brian didn't want a life with me, which left me feeling nameless and unhinged. I felt sick with disappointment and regretted eating nothing but sweets.

So after that I went to do what I was good at doing... autocross--which brings me back to the track, waiting for the next heat, just a few minutes away. My stomach is still churning from cookies, and I'm so nauseated I don't know how I am going to drive. I wonder if I should make myself throw up. We are racing at the vocational-school parking lot, and there has to be a bathroom around somewhere.

I run out of my car, leaving it in the line, and sprint toward the side of the building to search for a bathroom; Jessica is walking out of the ladies room and we nearly collide.

"Excuse me." I try to walk past her to the door; she pulls on my shirt.

"You're doing well." She's been dabbing tissues at her eyes.

"You weren't with him that long." I realize we are in the same speedy boat.

"Everyone knows that doesn't matter." She's looking at me.

"You *must* have told him," I get heated.

"He was listening."

"Oh sick." I'm so stressed I start feeling the violent need to race. My nerves feel like ice-pick pinpoints.

"I don't want you," she lies, sensing my intensity and baiting me.

"I miss Brian," I whine; she is breaking me down. I want to get back in my car.

"You're avoiding the issue." She's still looking at me.

"I don't want you," I reply. "Really. I told you."

"You're really into men?"

I notice Bill Zodiac at the parking lot entrance; I recognize him from last week. Jessica said he's one of the fanatics, probably walks the track in his sleep. I am shocked to see all the windows are punched out of his black Corvette and I think about the way he drove maniacally last week, razing cones like a lawnmower, and how it made me wonder if he was brazenly crazy. The AX man takes off points for wild driving, but Jessica said Bill still always wins in his category because his speed is so intense; his car looks like a machine of human will out there. Maybe his windows are broken because he cut the wrong person off on the freeway? Or maybe he did it himself in some fit of rage? Whatever--the funniest thing is that he still decided to show up at the race with his car like that.

"Check out Zodiac," I murmur. She's still holding onto my shirt.

"I used to love him," she confesses. "That's how I got into racing after my divorce, right before I met your dad."

"I can see his influence," I joke in regards to the fiery break-up scene at my Dad's apartment.

"Broken windows?" She turns to notice what I saw earlier.

"Interesting. Maybe he came by and asked my Dad for permission for a date with me," I clucked. "Bad timing,"

"Samantha, I need you." She's still melting.

"You'll find something else to fill that need," I shrugged her off, pleased by my own advice. "I need to get back to my car and move it forward in the line. I'm up again in a few."

"I can show you the world through new eyes," she says, and I think of the broken car windows.

"I don't need your view," I gush, my anger renewed. "I'm only twenty-four and I miss someone badly. Please stop this because I'm embarrassed." She finally lets go of my shirt and I walk back to my car; guilt and sadness are crashing together on some interior course.

As I near my Prelude, I watch as Zodiac yells at the officials at the admissions table to let him in, even though he missed the first heat. Someone points out that his car is damaged. He says it makes no difference, he needs the run. They nod and let him fill out the entry form. Bill gets into the driver's seat and pulls up behind me. He's in the wrong heat, he's not a novice, but nobody tells him that.

Then it is my turn again. I get in my car and drive up next to the guy with the wedding ring; I smile back at him and he waves me on. The AX man starts calling, "There's the white Honda; there's the lady to watch. There she goes!" I tune him out as I turn the corner, focusing in, gas to the floor, arms ice-tense, thoughts behind me, the road ahead, pure clarity, nothing but speed and coordination round the second turn, the wind in my face, my mouth drying out, the whir of greenery on the sides of the tracks, that last turn, perfection, my time....fifty-three seconds. My best yet. Thrilling.

I pull into my designated parking spot, heaving happy breaths. I glance around at the other drivers, the Corvettes and Beamers and Mustangs; one driver gives me thumbs up. Zodiac is already on the track, missing corners, hitting cones, and then he spins out and a few shards from the broken windows splinter out by the onlookers on the grassy knoll near the track.

"And the Zodiac DNFs!" the AX man declares, and then relays to the rest of us, microphone aside, "He's too dangerous. That's his last run."

This makes me the winner. Jessica stays in her car, avoids looking at me, but I get a hug from a driver in a Mustang from the intermediate category. I can't stay and celebrate, should anyone ask—because I want to go back to the apartment, to talk to Brian, maybe--except I know it'd be pointless, zero, because he doesn't love me. Pinching my upper arms, I remind myself to find a new path, maybe start looking in the paper for something in astronomy, maybe even just a class or two, and stay at Dad's another week at most. I recall my sadness and fatigue, which comes with an associated heaviness; my stuff is out of the Prelude, which drove great in the race, but it doesn't feel right on the drive back; it heaves like it is still loaded down. I start to worry I have really done some damage.

Dusk is beginning to fall and I see a few stars shining through spaces in the low clouds through my moon roof. I pull up to my dad's complex, and he is filling the lawn with new items again. At first I think Jessica has left some things, and then I recognize my clothes, my pillows, my framed pictures, my old schoolbooks amidst the furniture that did not fit in Jessica's car. Adrenaline seizes my chest and I speed toward the lawn like I am still autocrossing. I pull up with a screech.

"What the hell!" I yell, taking him on; I just drove against the Zodiac after all.

"I've been on the phone with my counselor all afternoon," he huffs while setting a folding table down on the grass, "and you need to be out on your own. This is called tough love."

"You're ridiculous!" I feel like crying too, just like Jessica did. All my things out in public like that. No place but the car to put them in. I am already worried I did damage with all the weight of the first trip, now I have to load the car again. My car is going to die.

"This is for your good and mine," he replies and turns on his heel.

"I can't believe you're doing this to me!" I yell after him, following him inside. "Let me use the phone!" I demand.

"I don't want a scene. My neighbors will call the police again. I will pack your things back in your car; I just think this is best for both of us," he says calmly.

I look at him and realize I hardly know the man. His face is strange to me, like Jessica's was. He was never around when I was growing up, always in some romantic hurricane with his new love interest. I always thought that was why he got married again and again, just for the excitement of it. He was addicted to the rush of being a newlywed. That first heat.

"Fine," I reply. I let him go; he along with the dream of knowing him that I had once hoped would show me a stray thread of myself that would pull my spiraling life together. I pick up a few of my things, my favorite pillow and my certificate from winning second in the autocross last week, and put them inside my car as the darkness outside deepens. I see Jessica's Siamese cat crouching under the bushes nearby and when I call, it comes to me. I scratch its head and put it in the backseat, thinking if I don't take care of it, it might just run away and die. And then I get into my car, and I imagine a shelter, not just for the cat, but for me, some apartment in the future, another college, it becomes clearer, someplace warmer, maybe back in Miami, lots of car shows, lessons about rockets and all things astronomical.... I am so tired that I decide to sleep in the car and finish packing in the morning, but the plans keep coming. I keep the moon roof open, under the sky, blinking stars, my hair becoming slicked with dew, and slide into fantasies of a future humming with focus and possibility; something aeronautical, I murmur, my head nestling against the velour headrest. I was on the right course, and soon able to fall asleep, dreaming of a fire-jetted Prelude.

Half-Hour Nirvana

I don't think he loves me. I mean, I think he does but I think he is scared, the way so many boys are scared of love and happiness. Maybe he is just sixteen and doesn't want love. I can't imagine that, but I am a fifteen-year-old girl, and we are very different from boys.

My favorite class is biology because my lab partner, Brandy, tells me all these stories about her older sister who's getting married, and the sister's fiancé keeps coming on to Brandy and she doesn't know what to do. And there's Brandy's four-year-old brother, who gets all the attention, and her parents are adoptive and reek like marijuana all the time in the little east Los Angeles box they live in (I went inside once and did smell smoke, but I couldn't tell if it was marijuana or just plain cigarettes). And one time her older brother and sister got in this fight, and her little brother was just clapping while they screamed and kicked and pulled hair and her big brother tore a piece of her sister's cheek off with his fingernails. This was the part where my mind kind of made a still of the story, like in a film where you can freeze the frame, or when you swallow something that stops in your throat. I guess I just couldn't imagine someone's cheek actually coming off and then I felt more comfortable with Brandy because I knew she had something to hide. Maybe she was afraid of someone not listening to her. I sometimes make stories juicier just so people will listen.

I tell Brandy all about Chase and I don't think the teacher even cares about our talking because he never looks over. I tell her all about how he took me home from play-rehearsal one night and I breathed his heavy cologne that I thought maybe he put on for me. Chase talked a lot while he drove to my house, mostly about baseball, and I felt thankful because I was heady and couldn't think of anything to say. I kept praying to God and Jesus and asking that this be the one. I didn't want to wait anymore for someone to love me. And I thought he was perfect. I looked at him while he was driving and he was so beautiful, all black hair and eyes and long crooked nose. I think it was his nose that made me fall in love with him, because I don't like guys that are too perfect.

I've told Brandy all this in biology; about how his skin gets dark and shiny when the moonlight falls across the planes of his face. I don't understand what more there is to want than lying in a truck cab, blouse open, breasts exposed, his bare chest rubbing across mine, my face bathing in wet kisses and neck stinging from hickeys. It was like my half-hour nirvana.

Chase breathed heavily over me that first night, making my chest tingle, making my heart swell, and nothing mattered in the world. It didn't matter that at home everyone thought I was no one. That Mom didn't want me (she had me too young, never found herself--I've overheard her yelling this at Grandma late at night). That some other lady stole Dad years back. It all faded into perspiration that fogged up the back window. I wrote Chase + Paige in the fog. He smeared it accidentally with his elbow when he rolled off me. We had four more times after that. Five times in two weeks. Two and a half hours of nirvana.

Brandy listens to all these details. She sends me notes when the teacher starts talking, sometimes gross ones with pictures of penises on them, all different sizes, with arrows pointing, "Like this? This?" I have to laugh, but to tell the truth (and not to Brandy because I don't want her to know) we really never did it; I mean, I saw it and it was out there, but he didn't go all the way. I loved that because I thought it meant he respected me, and that's so important. I know Brandy sleeps with a lot of guys, so I don't tell her this. I don't know why--I just circle the biggest penis and leave it at that.

Brandy knows that he showed up at my next play rehearsal and for three more and I have memorized everything he wore (the first night he was in a black flannel shirt and jeans--he always wears jeans). The first night when he took me home is how it happened, he showed me his hand with its calluses from playing baseball, and I kissed the palm and then his arm reached around the back of my neck and he kissed my face, and in a husky voice he said, "Hi," just after he kissed me, which was funny.

I went inside my house, a few blocks away (and definitely in a nicer part of town) from where Brandy lives, and I felt so wonderful and lay in my bed and couldn't sleep. I just relived that half-hour in his truck parked down the street, across from the golf course, where no one could see. I lay in my bed and could still feel the damp from the outside air, made wetter by the sprinklers going around the course a few feet from us. It was cold outside, and that makes making out so much better.

Brandy tells me she has to do the assignment in class today because she's getting all Ds and Fs. That shocks me because I think if you go, you can at least get Cs. I mean, it's not like understanding the universe. She tells me her parents are pissed because she's always ditching classes, and she tells me that her boyfriend comes over all the time while she is feigning sickness, and screws her in her parents' bed. I would think that was really sick except I know they are adoptive parents. When I went to Brandy's house for the first time, she walked in her room a few steps ahead, and with sly eyes dusted with the brown fringe of bangs that fell across her lashes, she raised her sleeve and showed me how she'd carved her boyfriend's name into her forearm.

"What'd you do that with?" The uppercase printing was blackened with scabs. Around the "N" in Julian's name a half moon of redness had fanned out over her skin, looking infected, maybe.

"Safety pin." She lifted her blouse, and I saw a heart drawn into her belly.

"You could just get tattoos." I sat on her bed and looked at her collection of colored safety pins in a Hello Kitty box on her dresser.

"You have to be eighteen, and I can't anyway. My mom," Brandy shrugged.

"I'll do it." I picked up a purple pin.

"Here, get it hot." Brandy held out a lighter and flicked it. She burned the edge of the pin's pointed tip, and I held my breath while trying to cut a "C" for Chase into my thumb.

"I can't do it." I exhaled and put down the pin, then rubbed my offended hand.

"We could be blood sisters, then." She offered her arm to me so I could cut her with the safety pin and mix our blood together.

"That doesn't work." I knew that wouldn't make us blood related and remembered about her grades in biology. I heard the front door shut and thought Brandy's mother was home. She was strict, an Amy Grant freak like my mom, and I knew I should get going. I didn't want to deal with that lady's crazy complaining—the way Brandy described her.

Brandy had overheard her mother talking to her father about remodeling plans for their '70s style decor.

"I want, I want, I want," Brandy had mimicked her. I squeezed Brandy's hand goodbye before exiting the front door quickly.

On the walk home, I just wanted to think about our times in Chase's truck. Ever since it happened, I've hardly been able to concentrate on anything else... not the school plays (so tired of not getting the good parts, anyway), not my regular best friend Tammy (she has a boyfriend and never calls me anymore, and she thinks Brandy is trash). Chase feels like the meaning of my life, when I feel meaningful in the world, in his truck, you know. My mom and grandma always said this would happen to me; they said when I grew up I'd meet a boy and move in with him. At six o'clock Grandma brought out Mom's wedding dress and tried it on me, telling me stories of beautiful boys and prom dresses and chocolates. Amid her rosewater-smelling perfume she put ribbons in my hair that fell veil-like down my back, and she smiled when I walked around on tiptoes trailing Mother's skirt three feet behind me. Grandma told me God had someone in mind for me, and I thought that's who would make me feel purposeful in the world, someone to love, you know. That's why I was on earth, right? That's why it's so bad that Chase has stopped coming around, because really, I think it's the first time I was ever happy. Even for just a half hour, I just was completely freaking placid. And I can't get over that. It's weird; but no matter what, I just don't want to go back to the way it was before. Just being invisible, I guess, being a listener, waiting for this God-given person to show up and make me worthwhile. When I took the dress off, it was time to recite the Bible verses, the book with gold-lined pages that told stories of sacrifice and pestilence and suffering, all for the love of a higher power.

Grandma told me the stories before supper. "With Jesus in our hearts, there is nothing to fear, Paige."

I was thinking of the one God had waiting for me. Where is he now? Does he think of me?

"We are comforted by faith because paradise is before us. All our sins are already forgiven."

What is he doing, Grandma? Why do I have to wait until I grow up to meet him, if he is why I'm here?

"And we are to forgive others as we would want God to forgive us for our own transgressions."

I'll be a good girl. I'll love everyone unconditionally, you and mom, everyone. Just let him find me soon, God. I'm tired of just waiting. Grandma, can you help me?

Grandma told me to have patience and to pray. And so I have, but it's been a long wait, you know, and those times with Chase were so fleeting, hardly satisfying. That's why I can't get over it. I can't stand being alone and waiting all over again. Chase rolled all over me and I felt human and more happily in my skin than I ever was around my family. You know, this is my love story.

But part of the reason I want to dwell on that happiness is because I haven't seen Chase now in two weeks, which is even longer than the period in which he was picking me up from rehearsal. And I can't stand to think of that for one second; I can't even tell you how much that hurts.

I have been fantasizing about confronting him and asking him why, which is hard, because I don't want to make him uncomfortable in any way, because I love him, you know. I love him so much, and I don't want to be anyone that might cause him harm. But I keep praying, and Jesus and God aren't making him call me any faster.

That's why during biology class, when I look over at Brandy and she's doing her assignment with lab goggles on, I decide to go up and ask for a pass. I just want to get out of the classroom, move around outside; I walk down the hallway and swing my arms to the side so they cut through the air, and I remember that Chase has geometry class, so I walk to the math building and stand outside the open door in the hallway. The teacher can't see me; I can hear him lecturing from the chalkboard, and Chase looks up and I wave for him to come outside.

I hate to say this, but I know he isn't too happy to see me. I can tell by the look in his eyes. I've seen it in my Dad's eyes, when I went to visit him last summer after I finally found out from my mom where he was. I knew there was someone out there for me, because I hated the boring world I lived in with my mom and my grandma, and I thought my dad was really who I was supposed to be with. But he didn't want me there. He had another woman living with him, and I think he thought it would be too crowded. The world is only for couples, you know, just like Grandma and Mom believe. There's nothing to do but wait. Dad lived in a small, smoky condo, and I left and discarded my dreams in his house, I think. They aren't worth mentioning. Really, I don't even remember what I wanted to be.

I am starting to get really nervous because Chase is standing here and he looks so gorgeous and it just kills me. He is in his baseball uniform for an after-school game and even has his catcher's mitt, which I think is funny. He walks with me down the hallway, and I playfully punch his mitt, which he kind of pulls away. I can tell it is real important to him.

"I miss you," I drawl in this voice I've heard from Julia Roberts.

"I have to get back to class."

It's a beautiful, clear day--hot and dry and perfect for being in love. I was so in love with him, I was almost drowning in it.

I take his hands and gaze into his eyes and continue to pretend I'm southern. "I can't live without you, darlin'."

"I gotta go." He pulls away.

His voice felt so terse, and suddenly I was mad; it was amazing like as much as I loved him I was just as pissed at him and I felt like his fist was clutching my heart so bad I couldn't speak; and I knew that if he walked away there was no way he was ever going to talk to me again, and I just couldn't survive like that, not like the way it was before he was there, and so I just blurted out, "Chase, I'm pregnant."

I think I kind of smiled when I said it, but he wasn't looking at me. He stepped back and put the catcher's mitt over his face.

"What?" he said through the mitt.

"I'm pregnant."

"Are you crazy?"

"It's yours. You're the only one I was with."

"I didn't ejaculate."

"What?" I asked.

"I didn't ejaculate. We didn't have intercourse. I didn't get you pregnant."

"Yes, you did. It doesn't matter if you did or didn't or even if we had sex or not, because even if you get close or not and just a little comes out, you can get pregnant. Ask the bio teacher…I learned it in Mr. Ramos's class."

"Bullshit."

"That's what happened."

He lowered the mitt a couple inches and walked away from his class, down the hallway, still not toward me. I followed. He covered his face again when I walked beside him.

"What do you want me to do?"

"I don't know." My head was spinning. I loved him, and I knew I was hurting him. I hated lying. I thought of Brandy, and all the lies she tells me (her sister's cheek coming off? Please). Her lies don't hurt me; she just wants someone to listen to her. Lying felt horrible for me, maybe worse than him just walking away. I couldn't stop now. At least now he was talking to me.

"I gotta go," he mumbled and started walking off campus. I stopped at the edge of the school's property and watched him get into his truck. I wanted to leave, too. It wasn't like I could go back to class. I felt like crying and strangely powerful at the same time. As much as I loved him, I was feeling that I'd gotten some kind of retribution for feeling so lost after he abandoned me. He was listening to me now, and maybe he would even stay with me.

But now I had a huge problem, because even if he decided to stay with me, I wasn't pregnant. And there was no way I could fake that—I was a mediocre actress at best. After Chase disappeared around the street, I started walking toward home. I only live a couple blocks from Chase, and I fantasized about going to his house at night and seeing what he does. I wondered what his life was like when he wasn't around me. I felt comforted for a while, even planned to possibly go by there that evening, and then I felt horrible again, because I'd ruined everything by saying I'm pregnant. We had never actually done it. How could he have believed me? I was pissed at God and Jesus and wondering why he didn't just love me and then I wouldn't have had to do that. I passed by my old church and dropped my school pass on the lawn. I don't know why I left it there; I just was sick of carrying it and wanted to be a litterbug, I guess.

After the church I just had a few more blocks, and I wondered if Chase was home yet. By this time I was crying. I wasn't embarrassed. All hell had broken loose because I was evil to the person I loved, and now he would always hate me. And if he talked to anyone they would tell him I was lying; it was so obvious. I was crying so hard I had to stop walking and went between two houses and sat at the base of the wall of one and cried until my stomach felt like it was inside out. My arms were wrapped around my waist, and I almost peed my pants. I sat there for a long time, hoping the stupid people that lived in their box houses wouldn't come out, and I was conscious of the prickly spackled paint that was digging into my back through my T-shirt. I felt like nothing because Chase didn't love me. I was worse than nothing.

Now I was this horrible person, too. I felt like the person my Mom always thought I was--someone unworthy of living in her Christian house. Now she could throw out her pregnant teenage daughter…if I was.

I heard something like dishes being put away from a window above my head, and since I couldn't sob anymore, I stood up, feeling dizzy and tired, and starting walking again. My cell phone rang, and I dreaded to answer it. I thought it could be the police or something saying I'd violated Chase. I don't know if what I did was illegal…maybe it is. My head was hurting so bad. I was approaching the golf course. The phone kept blinking, and I checked the display. It was Brandy.

I thought she was going to ask why I left class and never came back. Instead, she was screaming and crying, and I had to lean against the chain link fence and cover my ear so I could make out what she was saying.

Her parents had come to school and taken her out of class and were putting her in a mental hospital, she was yelling. She said she had told her parents that she was killing herself, so they were committing her that moment. I told her not to kill herself. I found it curious that I couldn't hear any traffic; it actually sounded silent, like she was in the girl's bathroom or something. But I worried about her, and I could hardly talk because I was so hoarse, but I told her again and again that I loved her and that she shouldn't kill herself, even though I'd only known her in biology; I knew that if she was calling me then she needed my help. I asked what hospital they were taking her to and she told me, and I told her I would call her soon and visit. She hung up, and I put the phone in my pocket. I was going to wait by the fence but then I wanted to get home before my mom did, in case I could call Chase and explain.

I was thinking again how wonderful it would be if I were really pregnant, and even dared to think of marrying him, because then I would be happy for the rest of my life. I knew that I was kidding myself, but I didn't care. I did that a lot, all my life, because it was nice to sink into a fantasy, no matter how unrealistic it might be.

My house looked so bleak and average, and I wondered how long ago that golf course was built, because no one around here was the golfing type. There was a large house on the same side of the street as mine, next to the course. I'd always imagined an old, old lady in there seeing me walk past every day on my way home, and that someday she'd leave me her house, and then I could see green from every window.

My house smelled like German shepherds because we had three. They ran up to me as I entered, and I collapsed on the carpet and let them all lick me and slobber on me and then I thought that I would never try to kill myself, no matter what. It's funny--I was not even really aware that it was in the back of my mind, or that Brandy might have been having the same fears that I was, that we were unlovable girls, unworthy, and even that her call helped stop me from killing myself as much as I'd stopped her by saying that I loved her, but even then, I think I was still halfway considering it until the dogs loved me, because then I knew for sure that I couldn't do that to them.

I wanted to call Chase and explain, but I knew he would hang up on me. I baked cookies in the oven and bread in the bread maker and nibbled on the loaf while I cut out a pattern for shirts I thought of making for me and Brandy. I thought of some slogan, maybe “Never underestimate the power of a woman,” which was on a T-shirt I wanted at the mall back in junior high and my grandma wouldn’t allow it. Or else we could call ourselves “The Undead,” because we’d barely survived our suffocating families. I called Brandy to tell her about it, but there was no answer, so I went into my bed and let my dogs climb in with me and pant all over my face and crinkle the paper patterns over the ratty blanket I’d kept since I was a baby. One was moaning, and I think I fell asleep because I was still sad and I missed Chase so much it was unbearable. I fell asleep thinking about that glorious first half-hour.

Beaux Fest for the Wicked

In frayed black sandals, I walked the length of Esplanade Avenue for the first time, reaching out with a smile, automatically--I'd learned from years of childhood scoldings to be a polite girl--to take the free lighter handed me by an old black gentleman sitting inside the back of a van. The interior carpet inside the vehicle looked battered beige, not unlike his skin, old and crinkled like a leaf that'd fallen on the hot sidewalk. He smiled back at me, just a stranger to him, no one—some stringy, dark-haired waif in a well-traveled shift. I walked to my newly rented room, flicking the lighter, burning my thumb while I pushed through the wrought-iron gates to the weedy brick courtyard. My anonymity cloaked me in New Orleans like a welcome coat in the rain I'd left far away in California. No one to call me names here. No one to know or hate.

But my nameless condition was deceptive to the memories that constantly threatened a sense of safety within myself; they were memories that fastened my identity into a state of despair that I wanted to vacation from in this hot-August city. My mind was my own worst torture device, sending the pleasant smiles of strangers to synaptic back burners while crowding the forefront of my thoughts with the horrible experiences from my last year of college. I walked through the empty flat to get to my white-walled bedroom, to lie on the twin bed pushed in the corner and hold back those memories I could sense flapping the curtains I wanted to keep over them. I picked up Toni Morrison's *Beloved* and recited, "Nothing better than that to start the day's serious work of beating back the past"--a passage highlighted in pink marker. I set down the novel, balancing the open pages on one knee crossed over the other, and leaned to pull my bong from its hiding place underneath the stereo. Using my new lighter, which had jazz radio station numbers printed on it, I took a deep hit. *The day's serious work of beating back the past....* Breathing out the sweet smoke, I glanced at the worn towel wadded on the floor that I had forgotten to shove it into the crack under the door.

Beloved made my problems seem common; I'd been raped, but I was only one person, not an entire race--still I had to keep reading the book to maintain that perspective. If I wasn't careful, the weight of my trauma became too heavy to let in much present experience, and I had developed a fear of trusting people; I'd lost faith that I could do things that would cause results that matched (in some reasonable degree) with my intentions.

I'd paid the first month's rent to Kandee, my new landlord, with a check mailed here by my mother. She supported my need to find solace, though I hadn't explained to her exactly what had happened. I'd been hovering in some hastily shoveled hole I'd found deep within myself, and my mother knew by my silence that I was closed down. There weren't long phone calls from me anymore, nor holiday cards. I answered questions with vague euphemisms. When I phoned from San Diego that I needed to explore the world, she'd seen enough teen soaps to imagine this was part of becoming a woman. For me, the idea of living on the border of the French Quarter overhearing jazz and cafe conversations about storms and voodoo was intriguing. If I'd felt more comfortable, I might have been inclined to talk to my landlords about my new city, but increasingly I was noticing a creepiness from the middle-aged people I was living with. I'd chosen this room because my pot-smoking and having a cat limited my choices. I'd found the ad while reading the Picayune Times in the college library back in San Diego; I was looking to move out of state after graduation, and New Orleans seemed so glamorous, so jazz, a city developed from layers of different cultures improvising on each other—I was bound to fit in, considering my mulatto heritage. I might blend in better in the South, considering how surprised my college friends seemed when they'd met my dark-skinned mother--my father remained a mysterious white face taped in the back of one of my mother's photo albums, eyes with sadness in them that I'd recognize anywhere; they were just like mine. My mother and grandmother raised me like two married parents in a little LA house I only remember wanting to leave. My high-school boyfriend, if you could call him that, had some experience with construction and built me a free-standing room next to our house. He did this ostensibly so I could have privacy from my grandmother, who kept the house up while my mother supported us by working as a nurse. Really he meant the room as a way for us to have more time alone. I appreciated the gesture, but I couldn't offer romantic feelings in return. Mainly I ended up using it to study, and when I got a scholarship to college, my mother acted like she'd always known I would, which was better than I had known.

Suddenly, papers were being pushed under my bedroom door. I put my bong back and waved my arms to dilute the smoke. The first sheet was a note from Kandee, who lived across the hall with her sickly cat, Precious.

"I know we don't know each other well but I have no real friends. I rented out the room becuse I was lonely. Ive never been able to trust anyone my whole life. The state took away my daughter a few years ago becuse I was an alcoholic. I have givin up drinking but they wont give my back my child. Walter and I dont spend a lot of time together. Want to talk sometime?
PS Are you doing drugs in there?

Kandee."

The remaining papers were copies of court documents describing her ten-year-old child's placement into foster care. I couldn't imagine Kandee a mother; she was a slovenly, well-fed woman with tattoos up and down her arms that illustrated all the signs of the zodiac. Walter, her boyfriend, was a high school janitor about fifteen years her senior. He'd been the one to show me the room, and I'd taken it because they didn't look like people who would mind harboring a suspicion about my marijuana use. I'd been using it about six months, and I found that I liked to keep it a secret even when it seemed people knew. I hid my bong, denied noticing any odd-smelling smoke if someone asked, and burned lavender incense relentlessly.

Walter had given me a brief tour of the three-bedroom house; it had a courtyard crowded with flowering vines and was just blocks from the jazz halls.

"This is my room, here is Kandee's... and yours," Walter had said while quickly opening and shutting the successive doors in the hallway.

Mine smelled badly of cat pee. Considering I had a cat of my own, which I had been carrying in a travel case ever since California, I decided to overlook the smell; the incense would help, and I could always supplement with candles and carpet deodorant. I quickly agreed to take the room. I brought in all my things, including my pent-up kitty, which I'd left on the porch along with some aluminum cans I'd been collecting from the sidewalks for pot money since getting off the bus. Walter watched me without comment, or help, and went back to his room after handing me the key--so I relaxed a bit in the courtyard, soaking in the sultry New Orleans heat--a little bit stoned. I soon learned I could hear the jazz from down the street during most of the day. Soon after, I took a walk by the cafes, looking at all the people eating lunch, living the normal kind of life I had escaped.

I met Kandee when I signed the month-to-month lease, and I was concerned by her appearance—sallow, bloated skin, inked body, grown-out pixie cut topping off a tremendous frame--and now, with the strange note, I was wondering if I had made an error in judgment. I thought I should speak to her, see if her gesture was anything to worry about, so I moved the towel aside and walked into the shared living area to find her. She was lying across the red fringed couch watching Montel, smoking, and her cigarette had an alarmingly large ash at its end. I looked for the ashtray--it was on the coffee table, amid several white circular stains on the wood--and handed it to her. I suddenly noticed the smell of cooking.

"I baked some enchiladas," she said.

"I read your letter. I'm sorry you lost your daughter."

"Walter takes care of me," she sighed. "Except for sex. He never wants sex anymore."

Why exactly had she wanted a tenant?

"He's not around that much," I said.

"He's into his science project. He cleans the campus and then searches around for clues. Don't ever try to go into his room without him here. Just a warning. He'll have your head."

This reminded me of the voodoo stories I'd overheard customers talking about in the cafe. This couple had been explaining to another duo about a tour they'd had of New Orleans ghost stories.

They'd been taken through graveyards and told about voodoo practices carried over from Caribbean islands; one of the stories they'd heard involved the shrinking of tourists' heads, which were later sold in head shops—very funny, I'd thought. Ha ha. Sounded to me like the kind of tales related to tourists because only the city's strangers would hear them.

I couldn't picture Walter looking threatening. He was a little white guy in his late fifties, I supposed, and he had the posture of someone who'd always worked very hard and had low self-esteem; seeing him had made me imagine that New Orleans was hot and unforgiving for the fringe, and that maybe I'd come to the wrong city. It seemed unlikely that a couple like Kandee and Walter had ever been able to get a place like this one in any kind of traditional manner.

Kandee enjoyed talking. She didn't ask about me, and I was glad because I didn't want to tell. I watched her monologue a while and smoke cigarette after cigarette. I didn't pay much attention; instead I listened to the rumble of thunder doled out by an impending storm. I wanted to ask her about it;

I'd seen the little icon on the bottom of Kandee's TV, warning of flooding rains. I worried about the storm while Kandee talked about her daughter's "jerk" father, and then my worry about the flooding blended with more worry about money because I wasn't sure how to live when my mother stopped sending checks. I had given Walter my mother's phone number when I'd moved in, and he'd gotten the deposit from her and all my information while I'd put away my things in the rented room.

I'd traveled by bus across the country, stopping in whatever places looked interesting, amazed at the wide expanse of countryside filled with people whose lives I would never again have contact with. When I left California, my mother had agreed to support me for six months, and then I was supposed to find a job, something in literature, which I had majored in--but I had not applied for anything yet in New Orleans. I thought about a job giving tours of the graveyards; it would be easy to buy a book on the sights and then relate the tales to the tourists, maybe exaggerate them in any way I found interesting, but I had read terrible stories about the crime around the graveyards, and some of the rumors about hauntings were pretty awful. There was one about a rock star who got HIV from a local beauty, and he didn't take it too well. He hired guns to take a sledgehammer to her spine, nothing to kill her, just to keep her in a back brace for the rest of her life. But she was dealing with the same news as he was, as she had just found out about the virus herself, and she died. He sped over to her bungalow in the Garden district when his latch-keys called to say things had gone awry; he ran into her blood-soaked room screaming, "She was ROBBED!" Supposedly they all hid her corpse somewhere in St. Louis No. 1. Then a few weeks later, when a tour guide passed over that area in the graveyard, the guide became possessed, just clutched his heart and died, right then and there in front of the group, next to a crypt. People from the tour started running off as soon as he fell to his knees, were gone before he landed lifeless on the ground. The rumors say it was her, so guides avoid touring the area, at least for now, until it's all forgotten. No one ever helps anyone, but I had to find a way to live somehow.

I focused back in on what Kandee was saying, and noticed the picture of her ten-year-old daughter above the television, next to a picture of Kandee's mother, who (she explained) was dead. "This was my mother's house," Kandee continued. "I inherited it after she died two years ago when my father never returned from Miami. My father died in a boating accident, but she thought differently. She thought he left her for some woman in the islands. Her heart gave out in this house, just after Walter and I moved in to comfort her. It always feels to me like she's here. What do you think?"

I glanced around and felt nothing but my melancholy haze. I thought of the hanging lamp I'd heard tremble over my bed the first night I slept there, and told her about that. My cat had taken the alert pose on the bed.

"Yes, that's her. Heavenly bodies are electric; they affect the electricity." She nodded and took another drag of her cigarette. "Do you want to eat?" she asked.

"No," I said, worrying about the safety of her cooking. That night I occasionally watched the lights for evidence of any paranormal activity, my tongue planted firmly in my cheek, while I filled my bong and read more of my Morrison novel.

Because I used pot to fall asleep, my dreams were often heavy, oppressive, and they were loud, filling my head with memories that were filled with the noise of crying. In my dreams, what had happened in California was transformed into something two-dimensional, like a black-and-white film reel I could play, pause, and rewind. But I couldn't escape the feeling of being harmed; it was chronic, even while I slept, and even nice men that I saw on the streets of New Orleans, talking and laughing with their girlfriends—in my dreams they turned sociopathic and untruthful and inescapable, just like my ex-boyfriend and his fraternity friends. At night storms raged, whipping my bedroom window with weak tree branches. By the morning, the thunder retreated, leaving quiet, incessant rain.

My head ached when I woke up because the pot had worn off; I opened my eyes, listened to the rain pattering against what sounded like tin, and noticed that another letter had been shoved under the door. I reached for my bong and took a hit before leaning forward to retrieve it. I picked up my lighter and lit a couple candles next to my bed before reading the note. This one was from Walter.

"Kandee told me she told you about the science project. That needs to stay in this house. We can talk later. Walter.
PS I never agreed to have a tenant. This was Kandee's idea."

Just then, an overwhelming chemical smell seeped into the room—I choked and coughed and grabbed my cat as quickly as possible to get outdoors. When I got out of the room I saw Walter standing in the hallway, looking unperturbed. I ran to the side door to let the cat into the courtyard (and she sprang from me, hurting my chest with her strong back legs), and then I yelled at Walter, "What the hell are you spraying in there?"

"Flea bomb."

"You can't flea-bomb while people and animals are in the house! That stuff will kill you! It's poison!"

"Doesn't say anything like that on the label," Walter replied.

"Yes, it does!" I was pissed. "Bring it over."

Walter walked over and handed me the can; he heaved a sigh to mark his reluctance. He was dressed in paint-splattered overalls. His full white beard had gotten even denser since I'd moved in. I looked at the label and pointed out the warning. Walter grumbled. It occurred to me that he couldn't read-- at least I wondered.

My cat was looking at me from the courtyard. Midnight, an Abyssinian, was crouched under the wrought iron bench. "It will be OK," I assured her. I waved my arms to dilute the poison. I walked around town in the rain, occasionally sticking my tongue out to soothe my cotton mouth and locking eyes with the homeless along Rampart Street. Four hours later I returned home to let Midnight back in and called my mother to ask for more money, leaving a message on her machine. Then I went to the closet to get the aluminum cans to bring to the recycling center a few blocks away; I'd finally located one nearby. My closet was empty.

I knocked on Walter's door. Several minutes later, he opened it just a crack.

"Where's Kandee?"

"Who gives a shit?" he said.

"My cans are gone."

"She'll come back. She always does." He shut the door on me.

My mom called back about a half hour later.

"Your landlord called me," she said, sounding upset. "Are you sure you're doing okay out there?"

"I'm fine," I said.

"She called me out of work, which I didn't appreciate, and asked if you were an alcoholic."

"What?" I exclaimed.

"She said she'd found a lot of beer cans in your closet."

"I was collecting those to recycle. I'd picked them up around the neighborhood—you know how New Orleans is a party town. I can't believe she called you!"

"I'm sorry I gave them my work number."

"Did you send a check?" I asked.

"Yes. But I would like you to find a better situation than *that*," she said.

"I'll start looking," I said and hung up quickly because I heard Kandee coming in the front door. When she saw me in the hallway, she explained that she'd taken my cans to the recycling center.

"That's what I was going to do!" I exclaimed. "How much did you get for them?"

"I'm worried you have a drinking problem. I called your mother," she said and handed me a book from Alcoholics Anonymous.

"That's ridiculous! I was collecting cans for money!"

Why did everyone always misunderstand me? I thought about what had happened at the university, all the stories my ex-boyfriend had circulated about me. I felt helpless to control my own identity; people always made up whatever they wanted.

"I thought we could be friends, but maybe not," Kandee said, and walked past me toward her room, stroking her languid cat. Precious never came out of Kandee's room except when Kandee was holding her. I suspected by the way my room smelled that Precious must have inhabited it before me.

I left and walked the crowded streets of the French Quarter, lamenting the loss of spending money. I saw tourists and college students, children and retail employees. For a terrifying moment, I thought I recognized some sideburns…grisly brown sideburns that stopped just below his ears; not like lamb chops, nothing dorky. Brendan was the epitome of shabby chic. He'd have a sandal break, and he could drag the broken shoe, walking lopsided, across a crowded fraternity party and look suave while doing it. He was always the man to watch; his confidence made him special, and I thought he was symbolic of my future, because if I had attracted someone so successful, that was sure to mean that I would be, too.

I realized I needed to stop blaming myself so much, because I knew that I feared that I'd gotten raped out of pure innocence, but now I could see what I'd seen in him. Maybe I wasn't that bad, and hopefully, someday, I could learn to trust my judgment in people again.

My buzz was wearing off and I was starting to get a migraine. That sick feeling often accompanied my memories of Brendan. I was nearly turned on, which made me feel crazy because he'd ruined my life. I was looking at sideburns like his, and I almost hoped it was him, coming here to tell me my life was going to turn out the way I'd thought it would during those days we were together--and that the rest had been an unbearable nightmare, like some drunken pool game full of eight-balls.

I watched the young man with the sideburns, who looked nothing like Brendan upon second glance, walk into a souvenir shop with his father. I had nothing to do with myself and considered walking the riverbank or down Royal Street, which I had found was my favorite, with all its blown-glass shops. Knowing no one in the large, touristy town made me feel invisible, which reminded me of when, in my mother's drawer, I first came across my birth certificate, the one that she revealed had been amended. It had my regular name on it, and all the other statistics were there as well, so I asked my mom one rainy evening when my ex-boyfriend was outside building that extra room, what had she changed. She sighed and cleared her throat, wrung her hands, then smoothed her skirt. Then she told me with flat brown eyes, mouth in a hard line that she had changed the name, because at first it had read, simply, "Baby Girl." She'd put my name in ten days later.

Baby Girl?

I didn't press her further. Her set face told me to stop hurting her. Later, when I was up in the branches of our backyard avocado tree, that seemed impossible--surely my mom would have had to put a name on there when I was born in the hospital. It was a lie, and yet I knew by the way she said the words "Baby Girl" that she was remembering it as the truth--and the only reason to recall such a falsehood like that was that she must have tried to leave me anonymous in her mind when I was born because she was planning to give me up. It was something she never needed to tell me, yet she had, like a confession cloaked in something else—like a parable.

Baby Girl's in New Orleans. A girl with infinite possibility: I could have been anyone, turned out anywhere. More than anything I just wanted to forget California, forget my entire past and the path that led me to that hateful relationship, even if just to be that baby girl again.

I returned to the house; Kandee was sleeping on the living-room couch with all the lights out. I was careful not to wake her and minded her cat, which lay across her wide belly staring at me with deep yellow eyes in the dim light. The house smelled of strange smoke, maybe pot, but not mine. It wasn't impossible that Walter and Kandee were into something unusual. I walked past Walter's closed door and went to my room.

My cat looked at me from my comforter, which was wrinkled; not like I'd left it. My eyes continued to dart, and I noticed my closet door open, a wet towel draped over the hamper. I walked to my bed and felt dampness on the sheets, as if someone had been lying in it after taking a shower. Anger settled in my lower jaw; I noticed some white paper under my door, which I'd overlooked when I stepped inside. It was an electric bill for the inordinate sum of eight hundred dollars. I checked the usage, and it corresponded to the amount, even though there were hardly any lights used in the house, and the air conditioner certainly wouldn't be enough to account for it. I decided to wait until Kandee was awake to confront her and stripped my bed sheets while my cat cowered in the corner--I knew I had to move out immediately, but I was anxious about having nowhere to go. I was considering Florida or Georgia, places I'd never been. I thought of Key West, where Hemingway had lived with his cats, but I was feeling a sore teary throat coming on from my frustration. I finished making my bed with spare sheets and put the damp set in the hamper. I looked over at the bill and noticed two red pills beside it on the dresser; they were not mine. I felt disgusted that someone had left their pills.

Kandee was still asleep in the living room, so I crossed to Walter's room and knocked. It took about five minutes, but he finally pulled open the door. He was wearing nothing but pajama bottoms. Walter had a tattoo of a naked woman on his chest that I'd never seen before. I worried that it was Kandee, and I didn't want to know what she looked like--it was like seeing them indecent both at once, and I averted my eyes.

"The electric bill is outrageous. Did you put that in my room?"

"I slid it under the door. Your share is one third."

"I have one lamp in my room. That's crazy. Why is it that high?"

"No one's business," Walter replied.

"Yes it *is* my business if I'm paying for it, which I'm not. Do you know who came in my room? There were pills on my dresser, a gross wet towel in my hamper, and my bed was wet. WET. I'm not putting up with this. No one would."

"I didn't ask for a housemate."

"Well, no one would agree to this kind of treatment. Who was in there? What kind of pills are those?"

"I think Kandee's sick. She may have wandered in the wrong room after her shower."

It seemed implausible, but I felt a little bad that I hadn't considered the possibility that it had been an accident. I was still disgusted.

"Not drunk, right?"

"No, just sick."

"And what about the electric bill?"

He looked at me with keen eyes, pale blue, like the bottom of a flame.

"Who are you running from, living in a place like this?" he asked.

"I just want some peace." I felt vulnerable and wanted some kind of ally, considering that Kandee seemed off the hook and I had not made any friends at all since the rape.

"Everyone has something to forget," he replied.

"Something terrible happened to me," I confessed to this strange man. I felt a lock inside me unfasten.

"Come in here." He pulled my arm. His walls were white--nothing hung on them. There was a large aquarium in the far corner, opposite a double bed set flat on the floor without rails. It seemed he let no one in this room. There was a pair of dirty socks on the floor and a tiled bathroom I could see through an open door.

The aquarium was mostly covered with a sheet. Walter pulled it back, and I saw what I had suspected earlier, a plethora of intertwined marijuana plants under intense fluorescent lighting.

"This must be the electricity Bogart," I said. "I'm not paying for it."

"Wait until you see what it can do. This is no ordinary plant."

"What is it?"

"It's from Haiti; I got hold of a tiny seed back when I was in the navy, thirty years ago. I've kept it alive. The essence works on your memory stores; it will make you forget your worst moments."

"Oh, sure." I stared at him.

"It's all chemicals, our brains. The properties in this plant work like pharmaceuticals on the chemical processes involved in storing bad stuff. It releases the past. Once you smoke it enough times, you don't remember it happened anymore."

"But it still happened," I said.

"Did it? This will disconnect you--think of your worst memory."

That was easy for me. I thought about Brendan, and the rape, and the people who taunted me because Brendan had ruined my reputation; I thought of the smothering injustice, the sense of having no say in my own life, the all-at-once blow of dramatic betrayal from someone I'd never imagined would do me harm. I remembered how I feared I was permanently unable to trust now (which I was testing with Walter) and that I'd lost the ability to believe there was something good out there in the world for me. I thought of how I'd developed a generalized fear of people, which had even bled to my mother, and about my attachment to my cat, because I needed to love somehow. And that my name was Hannah, and since I'd left California I hadn't introduced myself to anyone beside my landlords.

"Let me think about it," I replied. I could hear Kandee thumping around, then the beeping of the microwave.

I left Walter's room and followed the noises into the kitchen, where Kandee, in a batik printed housedress, was removing a pot pie from the microwave.

"Kandee, you left some pills in my room."

"Those were for you," she looked at me. "I take them for my depression. I thought you might like them."

"I don't want any pills," I replied.

"You smoke enough pot. What do you have against antidepressants?" She sat on the couch and scooped out bites of her steaming pie.

"I just want some privacy in my room. It's what I'm paying for. Walter said you were sick."

"Screw him. We're not talking right now. He doesn't like you either. You should stay away from him."

"I think things are okay with Walter--but I'm planning to move."

"What did he say to you?" She looked up with slitted eyes.

"Nothing. It's the privacy issue. I'm staying tonight, and that's it." I was making plans as I spoke, thinking of taking a train to Florida and asking my mom to wire money I could pick up at one of the grand New Orleans hotels. And I wanted to take some of Walter's plant if he'd let me, just in case.

"You can't leave. I need you."

"You can write me, if you need someone to talk to," I said and then went back to my room before she could say anything else. I lit up my bong, thinking the pot smelled differently from usual, and within a half hour another note was shoved under the door on the same paper Kandee had written on the first time. I didn't bother to read it. I threw her pills in the trash and passed out after leaving a message for my mother to wire the money.

I slept differently this time, affected by the sounds of the rain, like something had been changed in my mind; it was like I was falling through a weighted series of spatial planes, while going back and forth between good memories and bad ones. There was the scene with Brendan when I ran to him after I'd been raped by his roommate and fraternity brother. I was screaming, crying as soon as I started to talk. I was dreaming of the actual scene and yet the memory was inflicted by the pot, so the mnemonic image was deeper, heavier, sedated, wet even, like I was outside in the storm, drowning in floodwaters, and then my mind took me back to that frat house, where Brendan was beating me up after I'd been raped, calling me liar. I was seeing it all in the way it had actually occurred, but I was seeing it from outside the scene through a big window, soaked through the bone in the New Orleans rain. He was hitting me, threatening to murder me if I told anyone else, and then my mind slid down rivets of silty floodwaters, gliding over the city pavement and I was remembering how Brendan had ruined my reputation even while the relationship was going on—when he treated me like he loved me in a way that no one ever had, and I had trusted him, loved him so genuinely; it was still hard to accept, despite the obvious truth, that he'd been humiliating me the whole time, exaggerating our sex life to make him look like a King; I'd even discovered a lot of girls on campus hated me, girls I'd never met who'd heard things from Brendan's fraternity, because they thought anyone exploited like that was easy, someone to adore hating. I was someone easy to get away with raping, it seemed. Brendan had taken advantage--why not someone next? So I never told anyone what happened to me again--not the police, not my mother, no one at all; I was standing outside the window, the floodwaters filling up inside of me, watching the scenes, and then I was watching myself sleeping in New Orleans, in my bed on Esplanade, brought in as if pulled on a current toward another shore. I thought I had found the right place, sailing in on drugs, trying to forget my past in this eclectic port on the Gulf of Mexico. What past? What past?

The ocean was swirling around me, I was still in the dream, and I was rocking, feeling nauseated, like I was at the bottom of a ship in a heavy storm, and then I heard the voice: "You were always a good girl, weren't you? You were always a good girl."

And I tried to open my eyes, but they were glued like zippers, so I forced them, the blackness frightening me to a half-awakened state, and I was in the arms of a large woman, her weight was surrounding me--not my mother, not my mother, no, her scent was different.

"You were always a good girl." She rocked me.

I jolted open my eyes, and my room looked different. It was bright, the clock read about noon. I tried to remember what my plans were, why I was in this room, where my cat was. My eyes were having trouble adjusting to the light. I walked through the house, which was empty, but found Midnight in the living room. I remembered the strange dream, the one about my mother, and remembered that it hadn't been my mother at all. I didn't know who'd been rocking me in the middle of the night, or why I was in this empty house listening to jazz coming in from the open windows, but I was ready to get my cat and was thinking of my childhood home in California, when the phone rang and it was my mother when I answered it.

"Hello, Mother, I'm going to come back to California," I told her.

"Hannah?" she replied. "Hannah?"

Saving Mona Lisa

I'm running. It's cold out and the air feels hard and unforgiving. Underneath the cold my skin is slick and sticky wet against my sweatpants; my legs break into speed around the last turn-well, maybe one more, if I can. My breathing: it's getting stronger, fog freezing in my chest, but my metabolism needs this kick. I'm imagining the pizza melting off my hips: burn, baby, burn. My legs churn faster; I'm on the last lap. Well, maybe one more.

I speed toward the river birch on my left. The track looks barren, the trees all shorn, the cold having stripped their colors, leaving them dry. I'm happy to run past them, Nikes hard on the soft red dirt. The track is littered with my footsteps, after years and years of running here. The cold is like my husband's breath, always like he's been chewing on ice.

The trees line grand old Cincinnati houses built a hundred years ago. They've withstood winter after winter; they stand stoic, wind-whipped and peeling, filled with families that are never as happy as they aspire to be. I guess I know this, but I don't know how.

When I was young I wanted to live here and our house down the street is so close to my dream; only a few blocks from the track, those rich, autumn-glazed birches. But the falls have been growing shorter due to global warming, and though you'd think that means more heat, it's the winters that have been settling in, barren and unforgiving.

A shadow hovering near the old barn-style house starts to scare me. It's up fifty feet ahead, just past the bend of the track, a gray-like mass of darkness slowly, fluidly moving hither. I'm gaining fast on it. There's no need to worry: the police station just next door, air too cold to invite strangers out to stroll, but the darkness is too thick to be brush behind those birches, and that darkness just keeps….moving.

I pant my mantra. I will always win. Victory. One more round.

I'm breathing hard, my skin under my bra straps stinging, must be the elastic, tears collect at the corners of my eye. The shadow grows nearer, it moves, one step out, I see a head emerging from a hooded shawl; oh my God, he's out to hurt me.

Huge, plastic-masked face--male, shoulders so fierce.

He steps out with a switchblade, and I can feel it before it hits me because he's grabbed me and I can't move away; but I'm so afraid there's no hurt, just fight.

I will win. I'm bleeding, but I believe this anyway. I won't die. I won't die. I will Live.

Hard shoulders hurting my hands when I try to hit them and my knuckles collapse against his black sweater. It's raining cold, not wet, just cold. I slam my fist harder; my hair is caught in his hand, God, it hurts to have it pulled so much; I'll have it ripped all out of my head before I give in.

Fuck you! I scream involuntarily, And Fuck you! The words invigorate my limbs, I'm screaming Fuck you, kicking, scratching, my hairs are all over his sweater, we're standing up, he hasn't gotten me on the ground yet, I feel the muscle in my left side compromised, a side ache from running, oh but it hurts much more than that. When I notice it, I'm growing dizzy; God, that rush of pain is fierce.

And yet I'm cold and the cold makes me strong.

Fuck You I will win.

He's trying to find something, grasping around me, we are fighting so close. I will win. I will win. I will win. I will kick his ass.

And then I land on my back, he lands hard beside me, and without thinking I kick into his gut, and he screams, and after one more useless grasp at my chest he scrambles away, taking off across the parking lot. Now I hear sirens as my perceptual horizon narrows into a fuzzy little hole, like I'm alive but the world around me is half asleep.

As the sirens near, I turn my frozen head and faintly see the outline of a little boy in the yard. He's at the barn-house. Lives there, I believe. With his big black dog; they've watched me run daily. The house that is never happy. It is not my house. Grant and I, we do not have children. And then the hole closes.

In my coma I had memories of date night in our patio Jacuzzi. Carmilla and Tim were there, just walked over from next door in bathing suits, Carmilla carrying the champagne, Tim the cigarettes, and we were soon all in the spa. Foam filled the center of the tub, detergent from our bathing suits, I was thinking, feeling beautiful in the humid summer air while resting against flowing water jets. Carmilla ruined her cigarette while sucking on it, and laughed, so drunk. "It broke. My lips are wet," she said.

"Would you like another?" Grant asked, climbing out of the tub, and scratching my leg in the process by accident. So ironic--my husband, the obstetrician, fetching cigarettes for the neighborhood swinger; I thought of his anti-smoking posters and our pre-marriage kissing.

"Yes, take it away." Carmilla flung her free hand, lightly splashing me. Tim's hand rubbed up my leg. I tried to enjoy the feeling, but I could only concentrate on hating Grant. Who invited them here?

It was miserable, waking up in the hospital; my limbs felt loose and gummy and numb. The pain in my side was the focus of my consciousness for the first few days, even beyond the inevitable deliberations about the identity of my attacker—the pain was so pure and striking, like a muscle ripped clean in two. I spent much of my recovery alone, and finally had to stop wondering who had attacked me, because it was impossible to guess and only painful to imagine. I was in a thin cotton gown and wrapped in gauze about the waist. My head ached though a pillow was soft beneath my neck; Grant had put it there. My sight was marred by a faint black speck in my right eye, and I had the sense that I was in another person's body. I remembered everything about what had happened, and told the police as much as I could: the dark mask, the big shoulders, a glinty, angry knife, the barn-house and the little boy who saw.

Back home, wrapped in a soft pink acrylic blanket that smelled like Downy, I watched TV a lot. Quickly I discovered was quite the news sensation. Not too many joggers attacked in Cincinnati, not in our neighborhood. Not on our birch-lined running track, not on our snowy winter streets. One bit I saw on myself, on channel nine, showed this awful picture: I looked at least ten pounds overweight. I couldn't imagine how they'd settled on that one. I tried to call for Grant, picturing him sitting in our colonial living room, amid all the blues and golds and tans, or his nautical office; he was always at work; to see how they'd gotten hold of that picture, which I thought was from a Rotary meeting three years ago, and the blue shift I was in just one step from a muumuu. Grant did not answer, out of earshot. I could hear his sports radio playing in the next room, then the phone. He'd be off to deliver. All the crying babies he must hear.

Funny what comes to mind when you are unable to leave your house, watching naked trees through the windows, from inside your warm cocoon. I used to think that love conquered all. I had boyfriends I loved, before marriage, relationships that for a time put me into that "Nothing can harm me" phase, securely padded in some emotional layer of protection from the world. Leonardo was my lover in Florence, when I lived abroad for a semester, and I spent most of my afternoons learning Italian firsthand in the basement of a villa half-covered in grapevines. I never thought to dream that spring; the present was full enough to blanket any thoughts of the future or past. Now, in recovery, I found it hard to invest those memories with any sense of the real. You'd think you'd be happy, having survived a killer, convalescing in a beautiful home, married to one of life's winners. You have media coverage of your philanthropy; you have sympathy flowers swelling up in your hallways, steeped in deep vases, covering your dressers, scenting all your rooms. Yet the heater was too strong, and the pink blanket needed to be washed after so many days in bed, as did my hair, which had definite bald spots I had not examined. And I was alone and could not run. Believe it or not, I still wanted to run, and the pain in my side was incisive.

And Grant was as busy as ever, his radio going in the other room, outside or at work, taking care of me but hardly speaking. There's a strange caged loneliness to marriage, when you are tied to someone who doesn't love you, yet whom you live for. If you have children you can flounder in their dependence, drowning your needs in the martyrdom of motherhood, complain of too much work to do, too many diapers to change, too many dishes to wash, complain of a bad paint job on the living room walls, your husband's inconsideration.

But without the distractions, there is only you, the chatter in your head, and your husband's inconsideration. The loneliness is a glaring bulb without a lampshade, illuminating the bad paint job on your living room walls. Then there are only the walls. And the paint is everything. Fresh, ugly paint.

Funny that when he first got through medical school and his success was my self-esteem, I used to sleep with the radio in my arms when he spent nights at the hospital. I used to fall asleep to the running sports commentary, dreaming about touchdowns and home runs. I used to dream about our sons being track stars, our daughters being princesses. I thought we had the money, the neighborhood, the house. I thought the children down the block were auguries of our own. I'd keep in shape; our house would stay painted; love and money would be enough.

But there's something transient about attachment that can slip away into darkness, a moving darkness that haunts, that attacks out of nowhere. My shadow self, the one blocked by the identity I keep with Grant, keeps gnawing, kicking in my drive to fear it, to run from it, and to fight it, because I want to stay Monalisa Greenleaf, who I used to love being, the only self I trust can survive. Becoming this new thing, a jealous plague, a scratched-out oil painting filled in with sketch, there's so much misery to spread with your emptied-out self. I smoothed my hair with dry hands and knew I was becoming someone else; that Mrs. Greenleaf was already far behind, maybe for decades already, lost somewhere in Italy, slumbering on a warm evening.

Boulder

The Mercedes sped on interstate 80 through the Utah mountains. Pale ribbons of an emerging rainbow arched across the road in the distance and disappeared on both sides into the peaks. Sam could see how the Mormons came to consider it God's country. If Emmie had been along, they might have stopped and taken a look at the temple, jogged near Salt Lake.

Sam listened to the mild hum of the engine, wondering if Emmie missed him yet back home in Pennsylvania, or if she appreciated that he'd taken the time to drive the car cross country for her son in California. The Mercedes was a surprise for Terence, Emmie's youngest of five, who was just starting medical school. Sam could imagine the excitement the boy would feel when he got behind the leather-covered wheel. For Sam the feeling was anger. He kept ruminating about his argument with Emmie, who'd asked him to drive the car out alone to Terence because Sam had vacation time stored. But this was time he'd saved for a trip to Hawaii to see the Kilauea volcano, which he'd wanted to visit since childhood—he had hoped they would travel as a couple, especially now with the last of her children out of the house--but she'd persisted, imposing the air of dissatisfaction she knew bothered him most, and he'd relented, eventually insisting, as the date grew nearer, that he was happy to do the errand while secretly hoping it would earn him extra credit--some undivided attention from her, possibly a break from her long daily conversations with her children, which once was cause for an off-color joke he made about burying her with her cell phone cradled to her ear.... Now Sam hoped that once he returned from California, she'd finally take that trip to Hawaii with him--or agree to spend night or two in a honeymoon suite at Caesar's Brookdale like she had ten years ago. He recalled that ancient weekend when they'd reserved the Cleopatra suite with the heart-shaped pool and champagne-glass Jacuzzi. It was those couple of nights, polished clean in his memory from years of replay, that had kept him connected to her; that trip had showed him what closeness they could have, and he would never stop hoping--if he was a better man, a more giving husband-that someday they could achieve that kind of synch again. He checked his cell phone; she hadn't called.

Sam finished the soda he'd purchased at the last gas station stop; he'd leave Salt Lake City soon and could go all night on the forty-four ounces of caffeine. The nails on his left hand drummed the wheel, and he watched the landscape clear of city structures and unfold, once again, into open, dry land. The peaks crumbled down into flinty hills, and only one car drove ahead of him, a silver Camry with a California plate and a border that read, "Real women bleed silver and black." He tried to place the phrase, at first picturing a spider, and then recalled those were Raider colors--the team Terence would probably be rooting for soon, once he'd settled into his new place in Haight-Ashbury. Sam pictured the apartment Emmie had shown him online. Then he saw an enormous piece of rock crack from the mountain. It fell like it was pitched from the sky… a hurtling boulder—a sight that warped his sense of bearings like he was walking in a dark wilderness and was hit in the face by a bat's wing. The boulder crashed onto the Camry's hood, crumpling it instantly, and making the vehicle careen, screeching, across the highway, then veered back through Sam's lane, hitting the base of the mountain, and rolling over. Sam stopped automatically…he hadn't even been aware his foot had been braking while watching the mayhem until he was slowly rolling up to the crash, the car humming and his consciousness relating to him the sound of the Camry's door chime, and nothing else.

A few minutes later Sam noticed that the itchiness he'd been feeling for years was concentrating around his nose and upper lip. The Utah snow was in patches; one clung to the stony mountainside just behind a back wheel that was still attached to the vehicle's exposed underneath. Salt had corroded the metal under there, so Sam knew they'd come from wintry parts, maybe lived in Tahoe. His trance was broken by the sound of whimpering from within the compressed body of metal. The hood appeared crushed, like a convertible frame with no canvas top, the car of an amateur teen mechanic looking to be different. The wheels were grotesquely close to the ground. The boulder Sam had seen topple from the mountain now lay in large chunks on the road. The whimpering stopped for a moment--then it resumed. Sam attempted to swallow; his throat was bone dry. He leaned over and peered into what had been the backseat and saw a young boy's contorted face, wet with blood, his shoulders unnaturally hunched around his ears as he lay sideways. More blood was visible on the glass near his head, and Sam avoided looking directly at the two bodies up front--a fleshy mass of limbs, smashed glass, a shoe with a long high heel, just within his peripheral vision. Vomit threatened before he focused on the whimpering and the sudden sound of leaking gas, which threw him into action. Without thinking he began kicking at the rear door, fiercely, until he'd made a dent deep enough to use a wrench to jostle it open. He ran to his trunk--reaching around his pockets for his keys, remembering they were still in the ignition, pulling them out, forgetting he could unlatch the trunk with the switch beneath the driver's seat. He retrieved the wrench among a half-dozen crumpled maps and sprinted back to the Camry. The wrench was painfully cold, the strength he mustered intense, and finally the door gave, grating against the asphalt road, pushing the salt in front of it, and he reached inside for that mass of brown hair amidst the splattered blood and the flooding fear. Sam held the boy like a fragile doll and brought him to the Mercedes, ruining the pale leather seats. He called 911 on his cell phone, and when he found his voice—hoarse--he started crying for help, and inadvertently rocking, rocking the boy who'd not said a word.

With the crumpled door no longer providing support, the weight of the overturned vehicle compressed the metal structure another inch. The leaking fluids and sudden movement made the car seem alive--while housing two dead parents, their blood seeping out of the edge of the driver's crushed window frame.

After that, nothing more about the accident remained in Sam's brain. For a couple hours he was treated for shock, as he'd been taken by ambulance to the hospital to Salt Lake City along with the boy. Sam called Emmie, and she insisted she should fly in, but Sam said he was fine, really fine, and would finish the errand and fly back to Pennsylvania soon enough. Why he couldn't speak much about the accident he did not consider. He felt closed into a little hole, thinking only of the boy who lay in intensive care on the other wing while Sam recovered--but Sam couldn't bear to see him. The thought filled him with a hatred for all things little boy-- light blue, booties, all the elements he'd missed in life, because he'd divorced his first wife before they'd had children. Then when he'd met Emmie she'd already had her fill of childbearing, so biological fatherhood had eluded him, though he became deeply involved in his wife's family. He played the father's role well; it was something he'd always planned for--But the baby days had passed for all five--the youngest boy, Terence, was nearly eight when Sam and Emmie had married.

When Sam was released from the hospital that afternoon, he asked a nurse about the boy's condition and was told he couldn't be given a name, but that the boy would recover.

"Where will he go? It looked like he'd lost both parents."

"He'll be fine, Mr. Robinson. There's other family involved. He'll be taken care of."

"Did I save his life?"

"Had he a neck injury, he could have been paralyzed. But it was broken shoulders, but you did save him from death by shock," she replied with raised eyebrows and gave him directions to the exit.

Sam walked through a maze of hallways, wondering if he should leave the boy some money, and was plagued by the image of the hue of deep red that still painted the interior of his car that had been towed to the hospital. He got in the driver's side and grimaced, shuddering with unspent sobs, and then he began to think methodically about how to put the key in the ignition and start the car, about how long it would take to get to California. He'd asked Emmie not to tell Terence about the accident—he'd have the car cleaned in San Francisco and the child would never know what had happened in the Mercedes. He carefully obeyed the speed limit, keeping his mind on calculations of the time left to San Francisco. He remembered the ticket he'd gotten one summer taking a few of the kids to high school--an embarrassment--he was hardly speeding…only six miles over the limit and only that because he was trying to pass somebody in order to get the boys there on time. Aren't there better jobs for the police? What about all those new airport security measures... that'd be a better way to spend his tax money. Sam's tax refund had gone into the car for Terence, the only one of the kids going to graduate school. They all wanted to please her, he and all the children, but it was Terence who realized Emmie's deepest dreams—and the car was like a blazing emblem of success in every way, bright white and branded by Mercedes.

The wheel felt like money that Sam had worked hard for all his life. His brothers worked hard; his mother worked hard until she died. He'd played second fiddle to his first wife's secret lover and sixth fiddle to his second wife's five children. At home in Pennsylvania, he drove a Ford. He considered all this while he waited at a detailing shop to have the seats steam-cleaned. He still hadn't called Terence to tell him he'd arrived. The mechanic took one look at the inside of the car and looked back at him wildly. "What'd you do?"

"I saved somebody."

"The driver's seat will have to be replaced."

Sam got the quote, shrugged helplessly, and paid the bill. He rented a room near the dealership and called Emmie once checked in.

"I can't explain it. I think I had one of my hands up around my neck, like I was trying to protect myself, while there was this car weaving around, chaotic, I was afraid I was going to be hit...." He had begun to remember pieces, but his memories were slow and heavy. He conjured the memory of the bloody boy, and stopped explaining.

"Sam, you don't have to talk about this," she said. Their two dogs were barking in the background.

"I want to tell you."

"I should come out. I should take care of you."

"We'll go to Hawaii after I drop the car," Sam rushed. "You know I've always wanted to go to Hawaii."

"One thing at a time. Let's first get you well."

"Have you told Terence?"

"Let's not," she said, always protecting him from what she could.

"He doesn't need to know what happened in his car." Sam knew what to say.

"It was supposed to be such a wonderful thing," she said.

"Well, at least nothing happened to me," Sam replied. He felt a pang of guilt.

"Yes, thank God you're okay."

"After this, let's do something together... the Kilauea volcano." All he wanted to hear was an agreement from her.

"Sam, my job. The teacher can't be absent, remember? It's noticeable."

Sam was quiet.

"Another year," she hedged.

"It's life on your terms," he complained.

"We'll talk when you get come. Come home, Sam," she said before he hung up.

Another year. And he knew it would be another and another and another. And then her vacation time would be spent visiting her grandchildren, which were sure to come soon now that Daniela was married. He looked around at his empty hotel room, noticed some stationery on the desk and thought to write down his memories, looking for meaning somewhere in his life with her--wanting to conjure their dreams--and bring them back if he could. Two dead parents--he recalled a moment of the car accident. Sam felt so much emptiness, hollowness now clearly outlined in the aftermath of trauma. The drive out alone showed everything—he was just that.

The Mercedes was done in two days. When Sam went to pick up the car he noticed that the seats were visibly darker. He left the rental at the shop and drove the Mercedes uneasily over to Haight, absentmindedly wondering how Terence would react to the car. When he reached the complex a few miles from USF's medical center, Terence was standing out front and squinted like he was seeing double. Then he flung open Sam's door to hug and knock fists with him. Terence pulled Sam's hand up to help him out of the car and thanked him for driving out. "It's hard to keep a car out here, but I'll need it when I get my internship," was what he remarked once he found words to express his elation.

Sam saw a huge wrecking ball swinging a few hundred feet behind Terence. It hit the side of an already crumbling building, cracking clean through a brick wall. Sam rubbed his eyes.

"You look tired. Sorry you had to drive so far," Terence said.

"What was so wrong with Penn?" Sam joked, still focused on the wrecking ball. Traffic whirred around them. The sun was setting, the air getting colder.

"I wanted to be out on my own in California," he said. "Come in, come on in."

"No, no, I have a hotel. You don't have any space in there. I'm flying back in the morning. Emmie, you know, she needs me around." Sam looked at the sidewalk. "I could use a ride to the rental car place, though."

Terence dropped Sam off at the agency. Sam was fibbing about having a hotel reserved, because he hadn't done it yet, but he felt overcome by a feeling of distance to Terence that he couldn't quite explain. Sam drove to the other side of the bridge, in Marin County, and checked into a Holiday Inn visible from the freeway. Originally he had planned to tour San Francisco, but because of the delay, he only had one night left before his flight home. Sam noticed he was sweating and considered it a side-effect of the shock. He couldn't bring himself to talk more about the accident to Emmie either, whom he called on the cell to leave a message that he would see her tomorrow. He slept in the clean, lemon-Pledge smelling hotel room, left the sheets off him to try to cool down. He dreamed about the wrecking ball. Then he woke, and a willowy thought came back to him. Not a new dream, nor a continuation of the one he had just been having about the wrecking ball, he was sure of that--it was a dream he remembered from a while ago, before he had driven out. Sam couldn't believe he hadn't thought of it before. His sweat turned cold and he reached for the sheets, feeling like crying. The whole thing tumbled back like memories that had been repressed.

He was driving, he remembered! Driving on I-80, exactly how it had been in reality, and in the dream, he'd seen a boulder coming at him. He saw it tumbling from the cliff, and he swerved but couldn't get out of the way, and the boulder landed on his windshield, shattering it, causing him to lose control, and he hit the mountain. Crash--a huge metal jolt, his ribcage pounded against the wheel, the airbag releases. Is he still alive?

Sam felt like his insides were covered in sandpaper. He knew he'd had that dream before the drive. He should have told Emmie about it, to have proof. But he never relayed his dreams to his wife. Who did?

It couldn't have been just a coincidence.

He dressed and walked out of the hotel room, the key card lodged in his pocket. Why had the boulder hit the family ahead when his dream predicted it would hit him? He walked under the freeway and toward the coast off Sausalito. He had promised Emmie he'd fly right back, yet the thought of returning to Pennsylvania felt wrong when he couldn't find his bearings. He needed to stay a little longer until he figured out the reason for the dream. The ocean air smelled familiar but strange. He hadn't been by the sea in years. The salt air reminded him of the smell of blood in that car, and the cars on the seaside streets reminded him of the crumpled metal around the crying boy's matted head. He buried his face in his arms for a moment, trying to drown out the memories that flashed back, but he was presented with the image of the boulder rolling down from the mountain, and the way it rolled toward him in his dream. He walked back to the hotel and requested a late check-out.

Back in the room, which hadn't been cleaned yet, he lay on the bed and tried to put things in perspective. He'd had a dream--just an uncanny dream that somehow predicted when he'd seen a few weeks later, *no big deal*. When he was a boy, he'd believed rumors like if you put your hand over your face you will die in five years. That was the kind of thing someone might think who believes in the predictive power of dreams. He'd had dreams about volcano lava running through his childhood home, about wrecking balls... but he couldn't overcome his interest in this dream about the boulder and how a distorted version of it had materialized. He tried to remember the details more clearly…the Utah mountains, the flinty boulder, the chunks it broke into around the car…it was all exactly like his dream, except for the fact that the rock fell in front of him rather than on him.

If he had not volunteered to take the car out to Terence, would the boulder have fallen anyway?

Had he left for California two minutes earlier, would the boulder have hit him instead—or were those parents meant to die--rather than him?

Emmie would be wondering why he was staying in California, and not even with Terence, and he felt another tug of guilt. He began to concentrate on his memoirs- remembering how his first wife used to tell him he was a bad influence on her, because he married her and her dream was to be a famous actress, and she said she would have pursued it had she not married so young. She'd eaten herself huge because she explained that food was a substitute for love and he couldn't satisfy her. She never saw really saw Sam for who he was, instead saw him as some distortion of her father who she'd never respected. She'd left him without even knowing him.

He'd found Emmie through a friend at work where he'd found employment as a classified engineer and was making great money. She had been divorced for many years and while she had a good job in teaching, child-rearing was her true passion. He knew he'd be sidelined but there was a relaxing compatibility between them and she appreciated his art for helping out. He felt needed and loved--Emmie was the center of their home and everyone revolved around her direction, but while Sam felt a certain sense of "odd man out" lacking the bloodline everyone else in his household shared, it wasn't a *bad* situation. He always felt like he was striving for a connection that he couldn't seem to complete, while Shannon, Walter, Daniela, Gavin and Terence provoked Emmie's every need... but it wasn't *horrible*.

He flipped on the evening news, which only showed violence that reminded him of the accident. He saw a woman indicted for drowning her six children and a man charged with murder after abandoning his car on train tracks, causing a commuter train to derail and kill dozens. He started to wonder about the concept of fate—because he had dreamed about what something he later saw caused the whole world to appear planned and artfully executed. Had he been playing a role that had been devised and accounted for, saving the boy, being there at that certain time... seconds would have made a difference....

He thought of himself at that age, so many dreams, he was going to be an astronaut--it was written in his baby book, he'd scribbled it in at thirteen placing the book back in his mother's dresser like it was part of his life's instructions. He didn't become one, he now engineered materials for planes, but Sam realized he'd written it in his baby book because he hadn't trusted his mother would. He liked maintaining a certain distance from women.

Yet the mother in the accident, her blood all over her son, what kind of mother had she been...had he resented her, adored her, thought she would live forever, maybe even dreamed that when he grew up he might be man enough to marry her? Would her death cause an endless series of neuropathic synaptic collapses causing his emotional capacities to link up in ways unknown to others who had never suffered such a loss? Would his own life be an example of nothingness in response to the meaning of a trauma such as this boy's? Why was he saved, was it possible he was meant to do something else--or maybe--die some other way? Was there some design in how one died—and this, dying under a boulder—was somehow wrong for his life?

The hotel walls were white and painless, but his mind was spinning and he couldn't manage to sleep. He wanted further away from the accident. Not back home but further, maybe over the ocean, someplace he'd never seen that could devour his reeling brain, his emotions he couldn't seem to tuck back underneath. He checked the internet--Expedia, Travelocity, high speed was at desk and he could buy anything by punching in his credit card. Sam flipped through pictures of islands, some serene with hammocks, others with volcanoes, one erupting molten lava, yes, that was it—the Kilauea volcano, the lava that used to figure in his childhood nightmares before he grew up and became obsessed with the idea of seeing it with Emmie.

He clicked on the Big Island and changed his ticket to travel to Hilo on a red-eye flight and emailed Emmie his plans. He turned off his phone in case she tried to call and re-direct him, though he realized he hadn't talked to anyone in twenty-four hours and his throat felt sticky. He tasted blood and tried to cough into his hand. Nothing but clear spit--he must be hysterical, he reflected.

Sam booked a bed and breakfast near the entrance of volcano national park and studied up on the volcano. He read that it had been continuously erupting for over twenty years, that normally volcanoes erupted and then became dormant but the current flow on Kilauea had begun in eighty-four and showed no signs of stopping. He wanted to see the lava with his own eyes and felt a sense of excitement edging into his previous state of numbed-out-panic.

He arrived at the airport late that evening, returned his rental car, and eventually had dinner on his Mahalo Airlines flight--it took about five hours to get to the Big Island, and he passed the time reading the in-flight magazine that said there were a total of four volcanoes on the island--three were dormant, although it'd only been about thirty years since Mauna Loa had last erupted, the volcano next to Kiluaea, which let the current flow. He looked at the magazine photos of the red glow of the lava with anticipation, momentarily forgetting the sadness he felt under his ribcage from knowing he was injuring his marriage to Emmie and from his chronically-sickening sense of pathos for the wounded boy. He remembered the image of the bloody child and suddenly felt anxiety about landing, but he quickly concentrated on the details about the rental car he'd reserved with Alamo--which he methodically retrieved once at the airport, and he thought about the mileage on the Dodge Neon he'd been given while driving the forty-five minutes to get to his room at the bed and breakfast. The house was modest, surrounded by palms trees and hydrangeas and well-located on the side of Mauna Loa, just minutes from the entrance to the park at Kilauea. The owner had dutifully placed the keys in the mailbox out front.

Sam let himself in and noticed that he'd been the only visitor to rent a room, because the house was empty. He found his designated bedroom, marked by the letter A, opened the door, and smelled the musty scent of a room continuously inhabited by different people. He ran his hand along the antique Hawaiian quilt before snuggling under it on the queen-sized mattress and watched the stars in the distance through the large bay window just a few feet from the edge of his bed. He slept heavily, aching from the driving, flying and extreme stress.

Deep in the night he dreamed of the boy. It was the car accident; *this is it*, the boulder hurled toward him. The boy was covered in blood; Sam pulled him out of the car. Then Sam saw the boy stand up, and he was walking toward his bed, just at the base of the crumpled heritage quilt while Sam slept underneath it, not in Utah, not at all, the boy was in Hawaii, and Sam got up and hugged him, crying, "I'm *sorry*. I'm sorry that it wasn't me." And the boy was molten hot, his eyes burning red, down deep into the retinas like glowing coals that scorched Sam when he held him--but he couldn't let go, no matter how much he burned. Sam rocked the boy, sobbing, his skin melting in the boy's white hot embrace, until he could breath no more and his arms dissolved slowly into the abyss, which cooled like soft white cotton soaked in melting ice.

She re-read the story months later while hiking around the base of the volcano from a column in the Honolulu Star News—"A man dead as a result of Mauna Loa volcano's spontaneous eruption after thirty years of quietude; a sudden path of incendiary flow smothered a bed and breakfast and a hundred year old church near volcano village late Saturday night. Sam Robinson, a fifty-eight-year-old guest staying at the volcano's historic bed and breakfast leaves behind a wife and five step-children in Poconos, Pennsylvania." The summary read hollow—like an article Sam had faked. She'd been unable to return to her job after the news of his death during a spontaneous trip to the Kilauea volcano, that very same place he'd begged to take her so many times that it had become an image that haunted their marriage long before he left to disappear there from her. Emmie carefully folded up the article like it was made of crepe and put it in her backpack with the remainder of his things they'd been able to retrieve from the ruined rental he'd suffocated in: his car keys, a clouded laminate driver's license, and some folded papers scribbled with notes about what she could put together about the last few days of her husband's life. Sam was her everything, she thought as she looked at the mountain of earth she had come to face—her backbone, her rock. How dare you.

Kauaian Sunset

I used to walk barefoot on plumeria petals around my grassy backyard when the Kauaian monsoons swept over our home on the bluffs, before I had agoraphobia. I gardened and brought in mangos, papayas and guavas to keep on the kitchen counters for my sons. We kept our home-grown flowers in tumblers on the dining table; these lived longer those raised by the Hanalei florist where my husband worked delivering bouquets to our neighbors. One house, the yellow one at the end of our street, he often stopped at on his way home after dark, carrying any flowers that had fallen out of the arrangements. He lives there now permanently.

From one corner of my house I can see her porch where he currently resides, a view covered with denim curtains. Right now, I can see she's out there, smoking in a rocking chair, a plucky, blond thirty-year-old, tang-colored tank dress, or maybe it's just a long top, grazing her thighs. I prefer the watch the view from the window over my computer, in my living room, where I can see

Hanalei Bay. Normally, I pull those curtains all the way open when lightning fractures the sky over the bluff and watch the clouds move over the sun while water beads scribble all over the window. I lose myself in the beauty of the horizon, without a backward glance.

When my husband left for ten minutes all I could fathom were the Hawaiian hawks squawking from the ohi ‘a lehua tree near edge of the cliffs. I still hear them everyday, and they remind me I need to tend to the garden where my grandparents are buried; they were *haoles*, born on the mainland, but they inherited this property from an aunt of my grandmother, a native Portuguese Kauaian. My grandmother moved to this house and was widowed in her seventies, and at this point, when I was twelve, my parents moved over from Newport Beach, where I had lived since birth, to take care of her. That’s when I met my husband, a surfer boy, at the shoreline in damp bathing suits. He worked at the surf shop in the Hanalei marketplace, and I was wooed over shaved ice, usually rainbow; I remember the taste of colored syrup with salty ocean air kissing. It was cool to hang out around

Haena Beach and camp in a pup tent, loaned by Keanu's older brother Hiku, sleeping to the sound of waves and the occasional tourist's car driving by; before long I was pregnant. Then Keanu and I married in a Hanalei church which had windows of stained-glass orchids. My parents were there, tight-smiled, pissed-off, and underneath my white sheath dress was my first-born, Kamalo, still snuggled in my belly. I remember the feeling of that day, so much hope laced clean through with lust.

The gravestones are marked with scaly wings because ancient Hawaiians believed that dragons inhabited this area and that they guarded the sea caves used to house dead bodies while the spirits of the deceased waited to journey to the underworld. Now the caves are just tourist attractions housing the contemporary version of Kauaian dragons, the fantastic kinds that live in children's imaginations and songs, like good old Puff. When I used to sit outside, pondering my ancestors past, I'd remember the importance of the mythologies to their lives, their sense of reason; though my research has become internet-based rather than hand-me-down story, my sons still recall not to bring back lava rock from the Hilo volcano, it causes bad luck, and that those with Hawaiian souls know that haoles lack a respect for nature, one that will haunt them to be sure. For a while a few years back I was traversing my yard, making it to my Grandmother's grave, praying for a short period of time, and remembering their stories to me out on the garden: overhead hawks clawing at their empty nests, bees buzzing around the hibiscus. "According to legend, in life and even beyond, people are haunted by their own mistakes; we're told this by the ghostly return of loved ones killed by Hawaiian Gods because they return to play with unfinished business caused by human error. The ancient Hawaiians believed that if you weren't buried properly your spirit would not find its way to the underworld," my ancestors said to us, spoken to me through her. I have no idea what will haunt me yet.

Through the denims curtains I can see Keanu's wife is waiting for him at the end of the driveway; she is going to walk with him around the block. Seems they know the other neighbors, I can see them engaged in friendly banter when he meets her at the parking grass. He's in Hawaiian shorts, a tank, like her; looks like they are still surfing with sun-dried sea salt hair and shoulder tans, but they don't look young like me. Their older neighbors around Princeville are mostly millionaires who came dozens of years after my grandparents settled and died here on this bluff. I do a lot of work inside—cooking, cleaning, folding and ironing clothes for their various employments (which often switch). Right now I have a resort cook and a landscape artist. That might change, because my sons have no idea what they are doing with their lives.

Suddenly, I see an email from someone screen-named BlueSky, his icon is an iridescent wolf with certain dragon features, like grey scales and red-crescent eyes. Its strange limbs are neither wings nor legs. Lancelot Navarre, his face falls into place in the scene of my eighth-grade Spanish class. Lanny. I chased him around one recess and fell because the asphalt was slick from rain. One of my most embarrassing moments, I was once asked to list them by a social studies teacher and this one was high on the list. He asks how I'm doing, says he googled me and found my email address on my blog, says I was a nice girl. I google him. He's in Oahu now. Probably what prompted the email, two haoles settled in the islands. I reread his email: "Hey, I remember you, nice girl. In Kauai, huh? We are neighbors. I'm on Oahu doing real estate these days. I saw you are web-publishing your memoirs. Drop me a well-constructed line when you get the chance."

Yes, I remember him, his pure gorgeousness caused me to freeze.

I look up BlueSky's profile, but there is none. I google him again and see that he's listed quite a few properties around Hanauma Bay. There are pictures of him online. He's grown a light, scruffy beard, not too thin, dark-haired, when he used to be blond; his eyes are nice, big, wide-spaced. He doesn't smile in the pictures. He seems masculine; posing in one picture next to a large catamaran that I assume is his. Snorkeling…so many years since I've been in the water. Too many sharks out there, especially during whale season. I hear about poor surfers every year.

To BlueSky: "I remember you. The boy who always greeted me with hola. Funny you should write. I've been on Kauai since I moved from our old school thirty-five years ago. I'm as much a part of Kauai as the old palms I see outside in the yard. My parents died several years ago, and I live in the Princeville area with my two boys. Their father and I split up years ago, and he now lives down the road with his new wife. We have a great view of Bali Hai. If you've ever seen South Pacific, you will know what I mean. Thanks for your note. Aloha. Marianne."

I waited a moment before sending the email. Once it was gone, it was out of my hands, sailing like a message in a bottle, only through the tech waves.

I remember Kalle has the day to sleep in. I've kept his lunch in the fridge until he wakes. Kamalo's is on the counter to pick up on his way out. The rain is letting up.

Kamalo, my oldest, is taking a shower; the water's running. I glance at my computer clock, seeing he has to be at the hotel in twenty minutes. The Princeville is just a few minutes walk from here. I'm glad he got on so close. Kalle should be getting up shortly. He's got a light blue Beetle, the color of my hydrangeas out front. He was always so artistic. I hope he stays with this one. So much better than the prints he used to sell of vagina dentatas; they were psychedelic, vampire, and I hated them. He finally gave that up. Now he's doing beautifully designing our next-door neighbors' driveway. Kalle's already promised me he will not redo Keanu and his new bride's place.

Kamalo pats my shoulder as he walks by the computer desk and leaves for the hotel. Kalle is in the shower now, and I can hear the radio going from his room.

I go back to my memories, typing up my blog. That night I sleep in my bed without clothes on for the first time in five years. BlueSky replies the next morning. I am back in my chair, the same routine, my boys heading off to work, and I take the time to read it carefully, skimming certain parts, but internalizing others. I am surprised to see the email is so long, several pages. This is the part I dwell on. "I remember you too well. You haunted me. I wanted to marry you when I got older. I remember back in junior high how my dad began to recognize when I'd get this spaced-out look on my face, and tell me to 'get out of heaven.' I must have been warped by equating heaven with imagined sex with you. I'm still half-surprised to find you with two kids, long over being swept off by anyone. Guess I should have returned for you sooner?"

He also chronicled what he's been doing the past thirty years, sometimes in vague summary, sometimes in detail. There is no mention of a family, he seems to have been anchored by an illusion that his life would return him to me. He says he wandered around awhile and finally found his niche with land brokering. He is on his boat a lot. He'd like me to sail with him.

I see my role in his fairy-tale; it's as if my forgotten dreams are now part of a grander scheme that will lead to happiness alongside him. I'm overly-impressed, I know, but his words are so healing. I try to imagine life on his island, pull out dusty sensual feelings that I can apply to his picture, and the vague images I have of Lanny from my school days, long before Keanu. As I muster them, my isolation grows important, a mountain to climb and conquer; I imagine sailing with him, giggling at the mental rock video I have pictured, lovemaking under the deck on roomy Moroccan pillows.

I read more from him. "You've always reminded me of my high school girlfriend. I don't want to write her name, too sad because I left her and she died, by her own hand; this is a sickness in me. Her death caused something to die in me, as well. Mari, your face recalls a version of someone I lost and miss and I want to see you. I'm sorry my story is so bizarre. Am I explaining this?"

"Just tell me what you felt."

"I didn't do anything to this person," he wrote.

I'm sorry, and it's dense, though the sensation doesn't last; I return to my own jag of woes for the hundred-thousandth time. When I sleep I dream of his memory, but its a sexual fantasy, not her suicide, and then it switches to his nude outdoor sex with her dressed in only a little blue apron, and he's thinking "little blue apron" while he's remembering the episode while on the computer, looking at her old photograph, and I know I need to talk with him some more, that my unconscious terror is eclipsing his goodness, because he cannot be this way. "I didn't do anything to *this person.*" And I return to my bloody bag of sorrows; even with my boys to keep me company and my panoramic view, my life feels illusory like I am in a box that I built well, mahogany, but now I think of the dead girl's box. Glass coffin, all cracked up so I cannot see through to her heart-broken face. A house, a casket—both so comfortable and trapping and I look outside with open eyes and enjoy the view of the Bali Hai horizon, and it never changes. It used to be I stayed inside, buried alive in emotional loss because I couldn't stand to see my husband with his new wife around the neighborhood, you know, at the store or walking along the street. I wanted to be in a cave and have it over with, as if to wait for that dragon to come along and show me the way to the underworld, and if I had to go on living through this life alone, then I would wait patiently inside with my boys, who make me feel safe and contained. And then, after a year indoors, with nowhere to breathe, when I started to get bored, my boys brought home the computer I thought I had enough to keep educated. Eventually I forgot what it felt like to have the pebbles dig into the bottom of my feet as I walked on the open road or the silky wetness of a cloudburst pouring over my long hair. I lost the feeling of real life. My hair is still long, yes, like it was at fifteen. Long and black. BlueSky's notes are bringing on some thaw.

I wait a day to respond. I reread his note a few times, imagining his life, his ocean-air adventures, and what his suicidal girlfriend might have been like. What she looked like, a kaleidoscope image, her hair always black. I merge my teenage images of him with what might have been like she experienced, thinking of him a couple years older, like sixteen or seventeen when she loved him enough to die for him. I imagine loving him as a teen. In my memories, I remember seeing him walking down the school hallways in Izod shirts and blue jeans. Journey's "Stone in Love" soundtracks my images of an adolescent romance that could have and should have been but never happened. But I imagine it happened, like maybe we kissed out on the football field between classes, or that he met me at my locker, telling me how much he liked our date on the field while he leaned toward me with one hand poised against the metal door while I played with his school ring on a chain around my neck. I lie in bed and think about kissing him back then, and how it might be today, a silky wet eel-like tongue filling my open mouth. I begin to feel like I know him and think about how the ocean air would feel out on the open sea in his boat, while eating bagels and smoked salmon, maybe. Something fish. And maybe champagne.

After the boys pick up their lunches and leave, I walk to the doorway and look at the Bali Hai mountain, the ocean below, and the boats out in Hanalei Bay. I recall what living outside is like, and the tug of infatuation caused by BlueSky's approach reminds me that the restlessness from yesterday has not died. The nearness of the doorway makes me feel queasy, even the feeling of the dried paint around the frame while I open the screen flat back against the outside of the house. I see my garden is doing well; I realize am distracting myself, looking at all that natural beauty, and a few hours pass, I'm listening to Nene birds and Hawaiian hawks and trees in the wind while the air cools down into nightfall. I keep an eye on the dipping sun while I try to take a step toward the other side of the door, focusing above the pale fire that I know will fade into the horizon momentarily. But I feel sick, and scared; the feeling of the dentist chair washes over me so intensely that I think I might lose my balance. As I reach back to feel the doorway, the white painted wood, Kamalo turns the corner and he grasps me around the waist just as I start coughing and bend over, nearly falling back inside onto the nylon carpet that makes my palms feel itchy when I place them down to balance myself.

"Mom!" he cries. "What are you doing? I can't believe you went out there."

I pant quietly, looking at the mountains, "It's been long enough, don't you think?"

"Wait until there's someone here to help you."

"I wanted to see the sunset." The sky is broken into its usual colors; I want to walk out into it, straight off the Hanalei bluff to find Navarre.... My hand is holding Kamalo's collar.

"It's better we all stay here," Kamalo rationalizes. "We can all take care of each other."

I'm well aware that Kamalo likes our home on the bluff. The boys…they don't want to leave either.

"I might start taking walks."

"Where?"

"Just outside. Anywhere but near the yellow house." I'm shaking because it hurts so much to think about the outside. It's like sickness, this falling feeling through the pit of my stomach. I get up, and Kamalo closes the screen. We sit on the small couch near the TV.

"Some guests made a scene at the resort today." Kamalo changes the subject, nervously eyeing the exit. "A lady had a problem with birds, a phobia, and because we only have terrace seating in the restaurants, she said she had no choice but to eat in her room. Then her family got into the act, claimed the open seating wasn't sanitary; the birds might land on their food. The staff had to make up the trays, but then they didn't like anything we brought them. I couldn't deal with them." He pauses, knowing what I'm thinking. "But I didn't quit. I'll go back tomorrow."

"It's a perfect job for you," I reply.

"You don't understand these people. They stay there just to harass the staff. It's what they pay for. Everyone needs to stand on their hands. Then they want refunds. It's almost like a game. If it's not a game, then they're crazy; but the crazy seem to be into luxury hotels."

"You're a great cook. Hang in there. Separate yourself from the guests—their behavior is not about you, it's about their lives. They are depending on your effort, you know, for their sense of self-worth." I feel high and mighty able to help my son with such good words.

"You've never even been to the hotel."

"I've never been anywhere, but I've been on tripadvisor."

Kamalo laughs and goes to take a nap. The boys, they are so tall. I am their little mom, housing them all on a gorgeous bluff.

I replied to BlueSky later that week: "I always knew you would do something interesting with your life. You've certainly been busy since we last saw each other. I appreciate your openness in regards to how you've felt about me. I wasn't aware that I was someone you'd held onto in any way. I

am terribly sorry about what happened to you as a young man. I do wish you'd written sooner.
Marianne
P.S. Are you married?"

I shudder with nerves after I click enter, and the email disappears, instantly in his inbox. My hands clutch the sides of my keyboard tray. The rain is starting again on the window. No rainbows are out there, just the regular landscape of the big wet mountain filling in the window-frame.

I am partly amused by my interest; by the way I reread his information on google, and even do a search just for images. I come across plenty. There are plenty of him with another woman on a site posted with someone else's wedding shots. She is tall and dark-haired, and they have several children. The site is a few years old, it looks like BlueSky was the best-man and his children are younger than mine.

I'm painfully throat-constricted, but I feel directive knowingness, like I am doing the right thing. I trust my feelings of spirituality like my ancestors trusted their Gods, even made sacrifices for them. I want to step out again and listen (like I used to) to the men on the boats in the bay during whale season. If it was quiet on the hill, I could hear them holler to each other. I pull open the door.

"Thar she blows!" I hear someone cry from far below the bluff. The whales must be out there. The humpbacks may be migrating right now, though they don't usually come by this part of Kauai and certainly not this close. The breeding whales leave blood in the water, attracting sharks. Not good for the surfers next season. Not good for the boogie-boarders, either.

I don't want to try to walk out again after nearly fainting, but I am going to watch the stars tonight and stay to see the whales glistening silver in the moonlight when they breech. It was like BlueSky's stories have opened a door in my mind and everything is pouring out.

I receive the email later that afternoon after Kalle leaves for a job at the construction site, restoring the lighthouse over on the east shore. He takes the city bus every afternoon to that area around the wildlife reserve, working in vain against the wind and erosion threatening those ancient structures.

BlueSky writes, after several more pages of poignant, revealing prose (he's still been thinking about me), that he is married. There's no attempt to explain. I don't know what to make of it except to cry with my face cradled sideways on the keyboard, even though I already thought I knew and consider myself ridiculous for reacting this way. There was no romance between us; it was an hola, an aloha, a sudden wave in the middle of an ocean wake. Nothing to be upset about. I have my ancestry to go back to. I could get an online degree. I could even forget the blog if remembering things about my dead marriage becomes too painful. I could begin to go outside again and create another garden, anything to get out.

But BlueSky feels like the answer, even if just as a friend who keeps me waiting in the wings for more. I am comfortable with waiting, I've been waiting for Keanu to remember me for years.

And so I go out. I open the screen. The sky is broken into colors, just over the bluff, and the first stars are beaming into diamonds--and I cross the lawn, the gardens; the idea of searching for BlueSky compels me, pulls me out of my cave on the bluff, and I'm creeping down the mountain, my fingers scratching on red rock, flint gouging under my nails. I'm dangling, still holding on, yet my soul is elsewhere, somewhere over the water, to another island, into some limelit, sunset place that is neither here nor there, but is somewhere out in the natural wild that I can find.

My eyes are closed, so much distance to the water, and then I feel the wind blow from the sails, and I can see BlueSky's sailboat coming over the sea. The ship comes closer, I reach down, whipping into tomorrow, winds like jaws of steel, he gathers a rope, slings it up to the cliff, and I crawl downward, onto the mast. Oh my God, it's him, I hug his blue sweater, fall lightly onto the mast in his embrace, mildly intoxicated by his reality, I wonder if we should kiss, he sees this in my face but he only kisses my nose. I find my footing on the bow of the ship, and slide down holding onto the sail, we sail over to the cave, where I see some shining shadows that we approach, and I feel the wind blowing through me, around me, nearly hurricane-charged.

"Cross over," he assists me into the dark shadows, and I can see a wall of shining scales in the distance, my stomach clutches, the stench of blood, the shining long teeth protrude from a silvery serpentine dragon.

"Oh, oh my God," I try to turn back.

Its eyes are pearly-white half-moons, watching me with interest; it doesn't move. "Please stay," it utters; I can't tell if the foggy-voice is the creature's or BlueSky's for a moment. I don't know why he's taken me here, BlueSky, if I'm the dragon's prey, but I feel, no, BlueSky's dark power is versus my true heart; I'd imagined love/ freedom/ power/ islands of love lace clouds, but he is an ice-cavern self... narcissistic, no humanity.

I'm still, having drifted from the false assurance of BlueSky's arm, I'm narrowing down into the feeling of light, transparent, flammable, but I can still see the serpentine dragon through a dim sheen, nursing a baby, teeth bloodstained from eating a cadaver long-since abandoned. I step over corpses in various states of decay, the air smells metallic.

I loved the blue and the Corona lime smell of you salty like ocean air kissing

Snow cone rainbow stain all over spring garden gravestones sky going dusky under stars set aglow by full moonlight

If it's curtain call, I can't tell, I look for this dragon, BlueSky my love, prince charming, who took me over the Ocean of Styx full of lost bodies, wind full of decay, my grandmother's eyes in a serpentine dragon's face. My love, his hand rough like scales shifting me through cool waters, the cave's floor is wet with melting stalagmites, mixed with rotting flesh, seeping through my skin the enemy if this is humanity dark waters full of sleaze, bloodless remains.

He's handsome, so attractive, so soft when the wind stops, he's wolfen, my eyes closed, I can feel my wings, worlds turning, crystal wood high in the air, a tree branch underneath me; I make no sense, humanity, is not an act, it's a faith. Ladyhawke.

I'm safe. Flying overseas toward the Ihalani Palace, love so lost, but I'm safe, and its pink, trestles, roses, sweet smelling pikake, bamboo leaves scent my feathers, my voice a hacking slither that lilts through my soul. Still; all mine.

The wolf is on the river bank in Kauai that glides by the other side of the cave; wooly grey cape, his eyes glittery almonds that glance upward because he can hear any rustle, any near silent breath, his mouth is bloody. I have the sense that he mauled the dragon, escaped back to the ship, had walked across his wife's blood-drenched carcass (has he gone mad?) that is lying underneath the deck. Not knowing I was a Goddess, he has had some bad luck. I understood who I was, when I was transferred into safety by the dragon, by nature of my true love, to save me from an inhumane man, but that I would return to my children; not as Ladyhawke, but in my human form; my wolf will roam alone, feeding like a vulture forever, and I will never see him again.

"Navarre...," my voice rattles through the wind and he can hear it; he looks skyward, wolf eyes, so beautiful, feeling; tasting thick blood.

What he did
Now tell me
Whispering in the trees
His thoughts are in my thoughts
He killed her for her lucky heart

Her mere decency

Her ticket to life

And he thought mine would bring him Eternity

What many men have lost

In death and love and reason

Acknowledgements

Thank you to my beautiful son Darren, my mother, my sister, my extended family, my wonderful friends, especially my sister-in-Christ Heather Carno Riley, and my longtime amies Peggie Dougherty Gonyea, Shannon Crawford Donnan, Pamela Brandt Shikiar, Raquel Ogren Re, Lee Fallon and Victoria Kersthold Beliso, and to some special people who have helped or been inspirational along the way: Alexander Hallak, Richard Fantina, Ron Samul, Tamar Heller, Michael Griffith, Jim Schiff, Jana Braziel, Beth Ash, Karen Anijar, Helen Dunn, Teresa Jones-Haney, Misty York Elsasser, Alice Tsai-Secker, Dalora Clark, Ted Lutter, Darcy Jones, Michelle Coletta, Holly Kniss, George Saunders, Oprah Winfrey, Tim Burton, Derek Frey, Jim and Cecilia Lentz, Rick Borsini, James Hetfield, Lars Ulrich, Kirk Hammett, Jason Newsted, Dylan Conroy, Matt Ragghianti, Dave Roberts, Steve Quarles, Guillermo Shuton, Robert Danila, Darrin Doyle, Chris Hay, Darren Bayless, Jody Bates, Madhu Sinha, Saverio Tomaiuolo, Elizabeth Anderman, Judith Sanders, Julie Barst, Jennifer Beauvais, Nick

Harris, Maria Granic-White, Kate Holterhoff, Stephanie King, Laurence Talairach-Vielmas, Johanna Vanderspool, Brown Crown Media, Gloria Allred, and Julia Kristeva.

Of course, many thanks to Mary Wollstonecraft, Mary Shelley, and Emily Bronte for their deeply influential art, and as always, thank you to my beloved authorial heroine, Joyce Carol Oates.

Marilyn Brock

Dr. Marilyn Brock is a literary critic and fiction writer. She was born in Whittier, California and was the eldest granddaughter of a locally famous protestant minister. Her grandmother's family migrated from France, near the Black Forest, and she was involved with philanthropy. Marilyn Brock's father served in the US Air Force and her mother taught junior high school in the Los Angeles area. Marilyn Brock spends most of her time writing, surfing, horseback riding, practicing yoga and otherwise enjoying life on the coast in

Huntington Beach, California, with her ten-year-old son Darren. Previous residences include Paris, France, Quebec City, Canada and Blue Ash, Ohio. She is very interested in globalization and its related opportunities for peace and the environment. She has a PhD in English and Comparative Literature from the University of Cincinnati, where her studies focused on Victorian literature, Psychoanalytic, Feminist and Race Theory and Twentieth Century American literature with an emphasis on the Gothic. She presented "The Vamp and the Good English Mother: Female Roles in Le Fanu's *Carmilla* and Stoker's *Dracula*" at the 2003 NEMLA conference in Pennsylvania and has published short fiction in Miranda Literary Magazine, SN Review, Planet Magazine and other literary journals. She is the editor and a contributing author of a literary anthology titled *From Wollstonecraft to Stoker: Essays on Gothic and Victorian Sensation Fiction* published in 2009 by McFarland Press. *Beaux Fest for the Wicked* is her first published collection of stories.

www.ingramcontent.com/pod-product-compliance
Lightning Source LLC
LaVergne TN
LVHW020540100826
845148LV00010B/1555